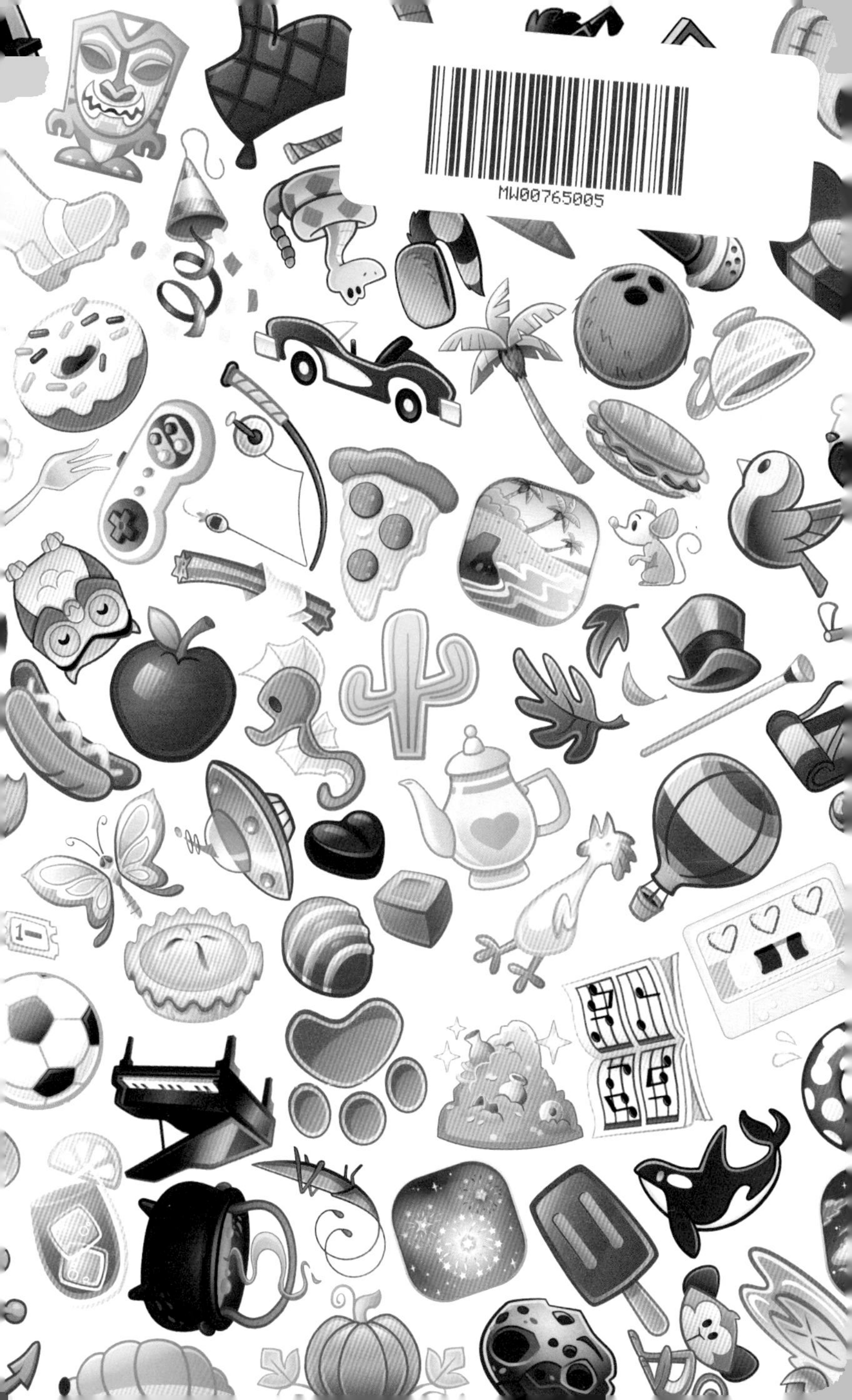

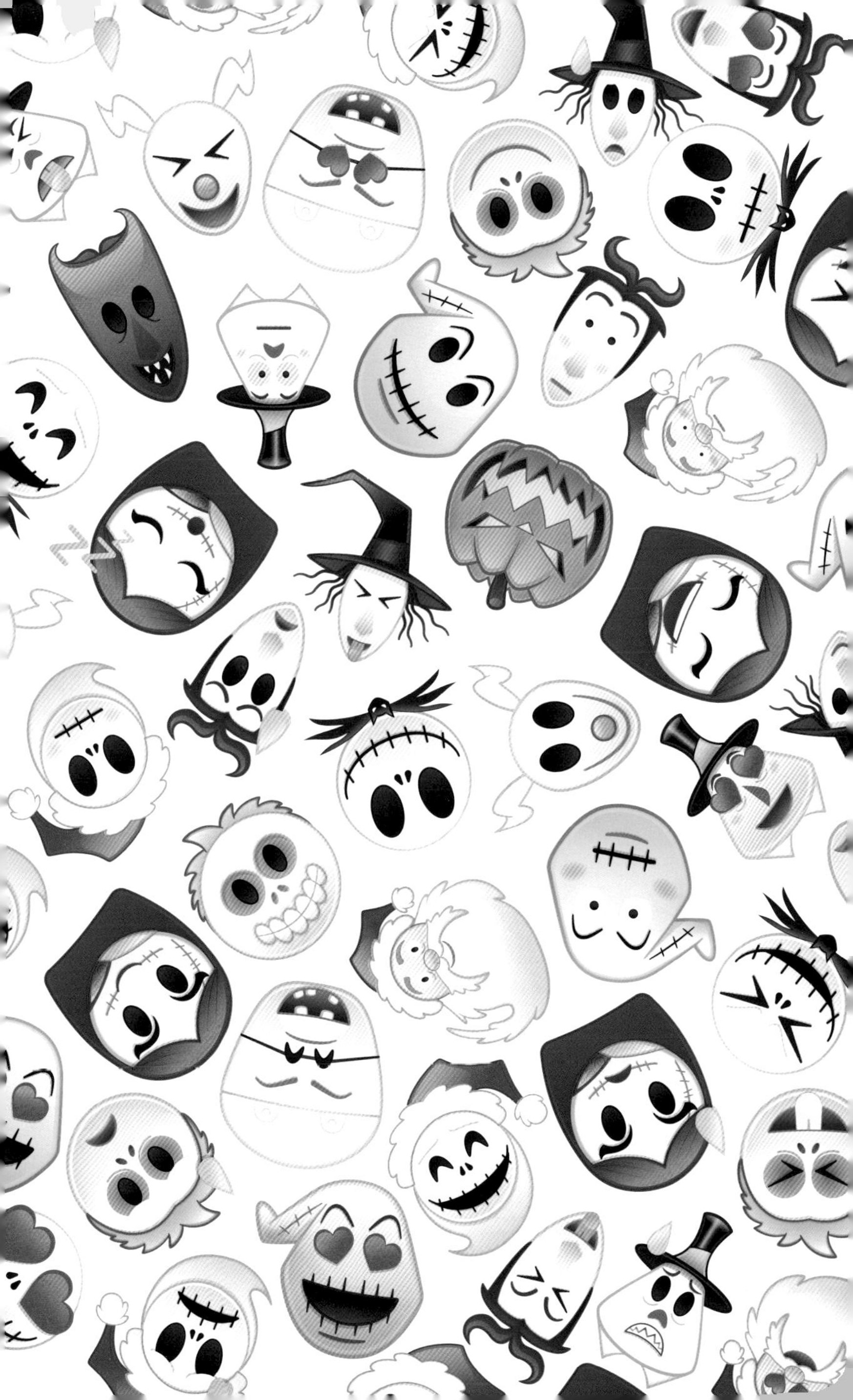

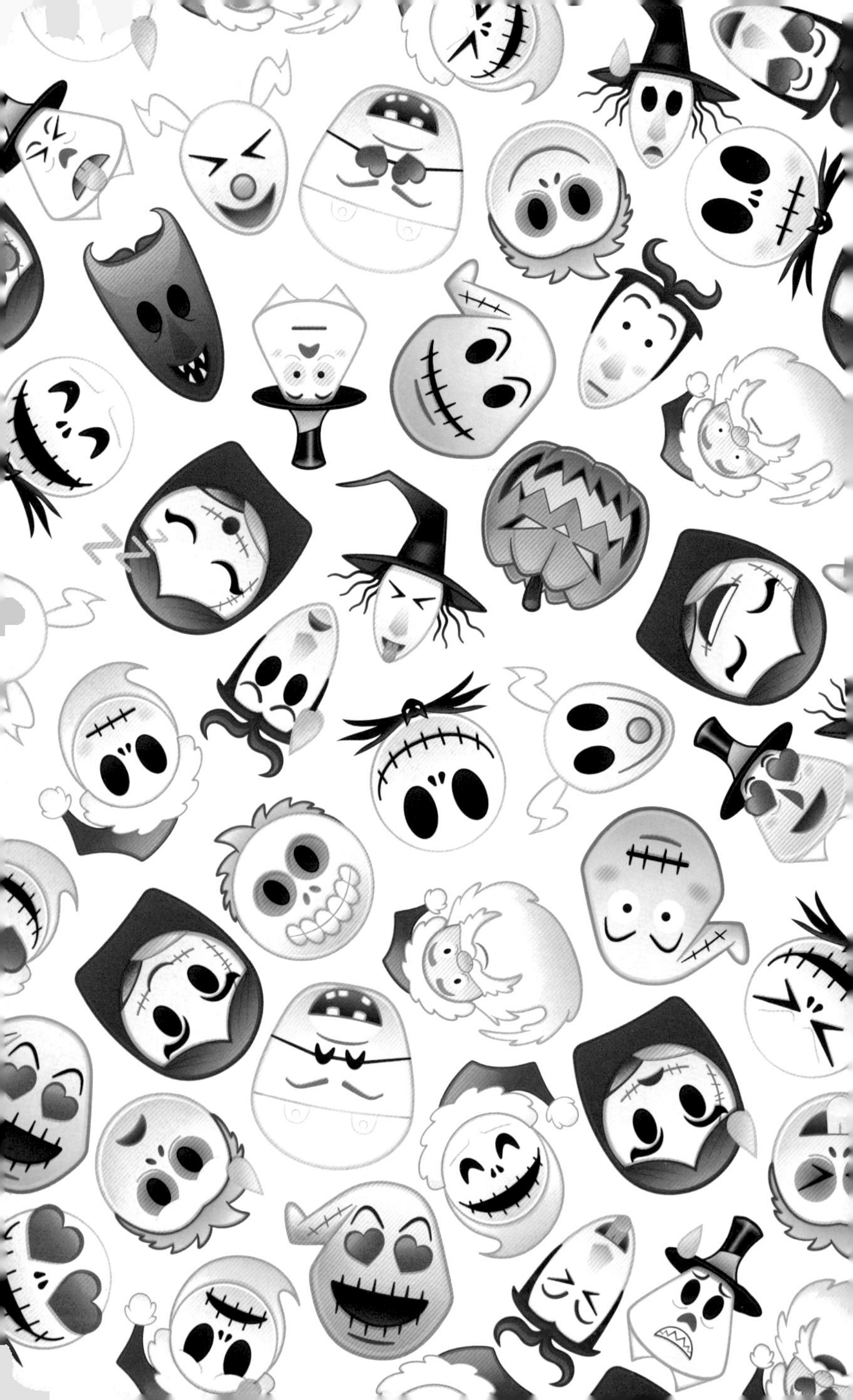

Disney

Tim Burton's The Nightmare Before Christmas

As Told By Disney emoji

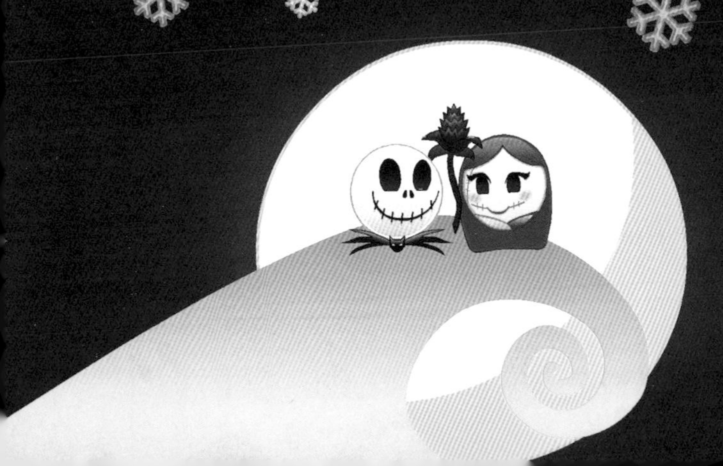

JOE BOOKS

Published simultaneously in the United States and Canada by
Joe Books Ltd,
489 College Street, Suite 203, Toronto, ON M6G 1A5

www.joebooks.com

First Joe Books edition: September 2017

Print ISBN: 978-1-77275-534-3

ebook ISBN: 978-1-77275-788-0

Library and Archives Canada Cataloguing in Publication
information is available upon request

Printed and bound in Canada
1 3 5 7 9 10 8 6 4 2

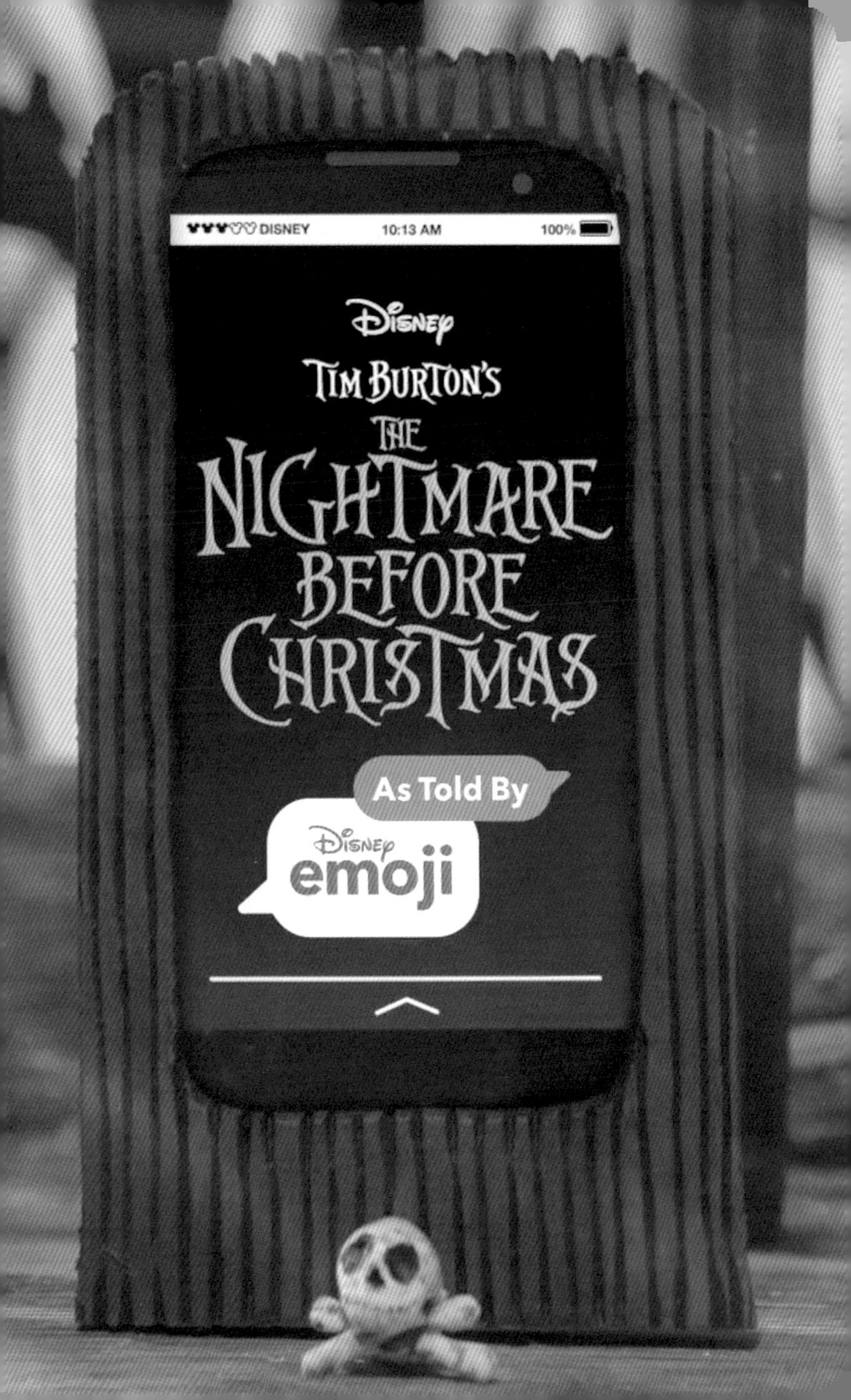
DISNEY
10:13 AM
100%
Disney
Tim Burton's
The Nightmare Before Christmas
As Told By
Disney
emoji

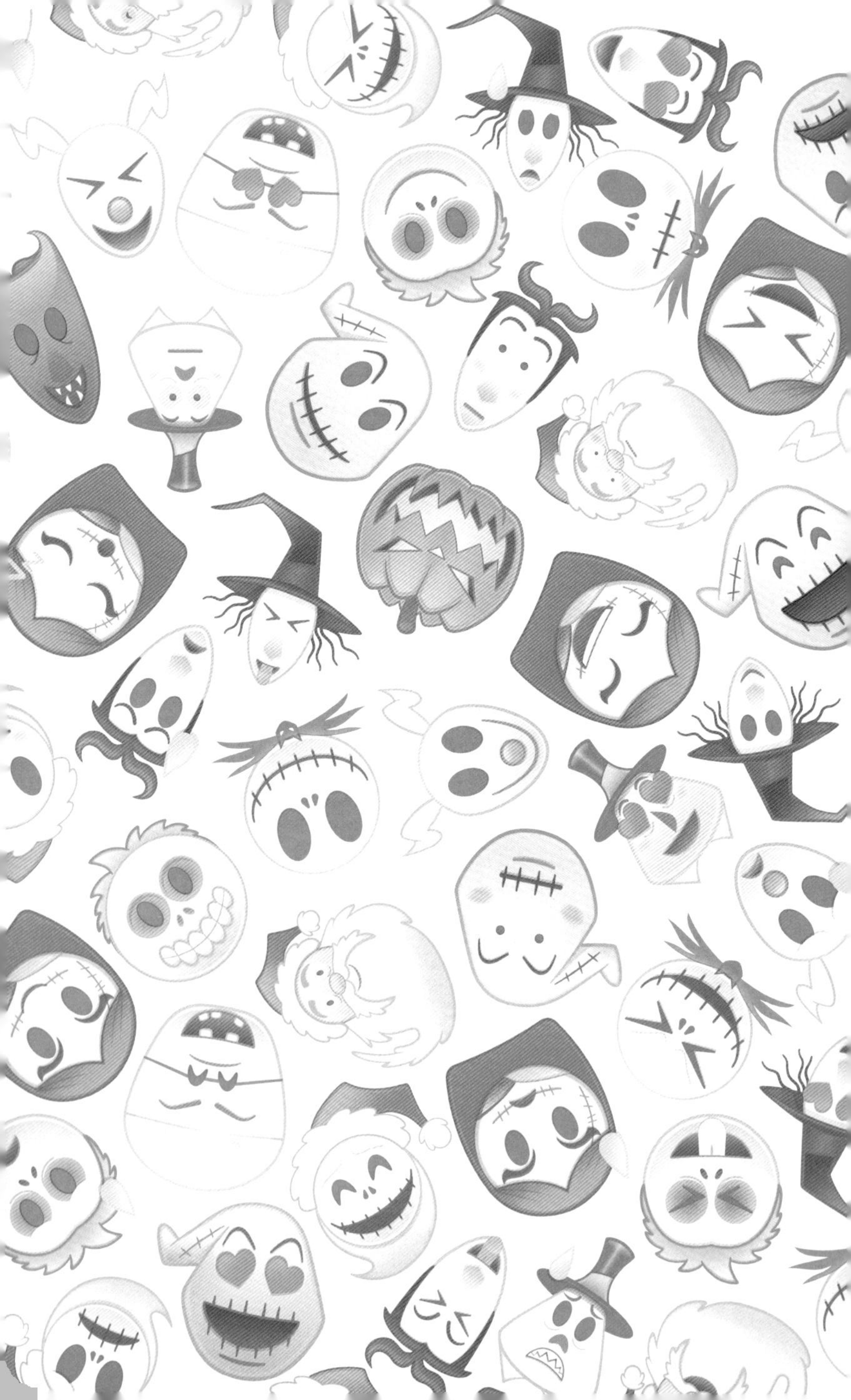

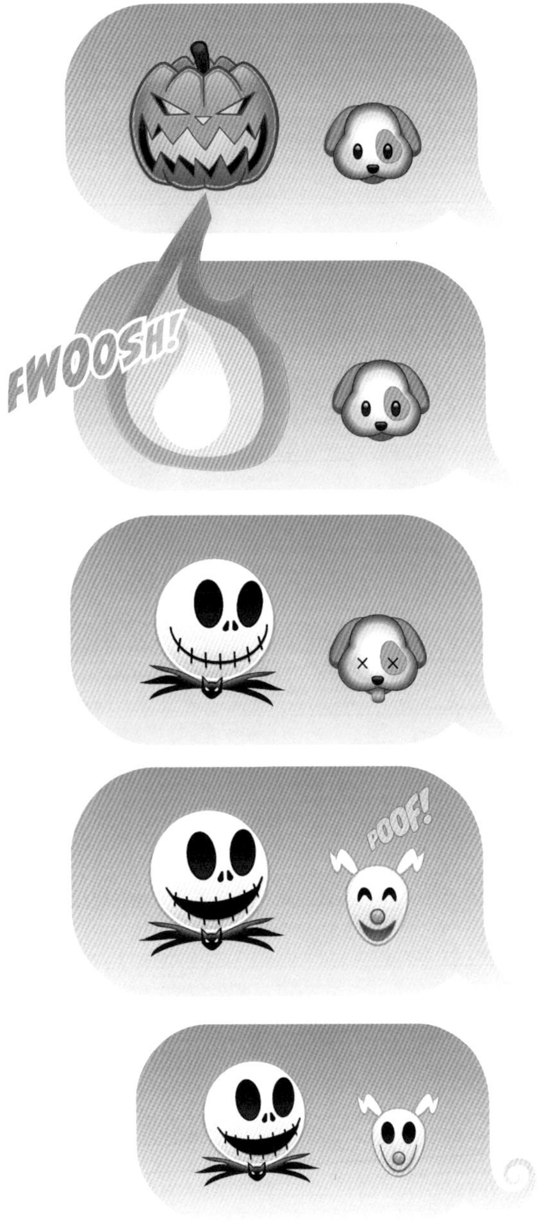
FWOOSH!
POOF!

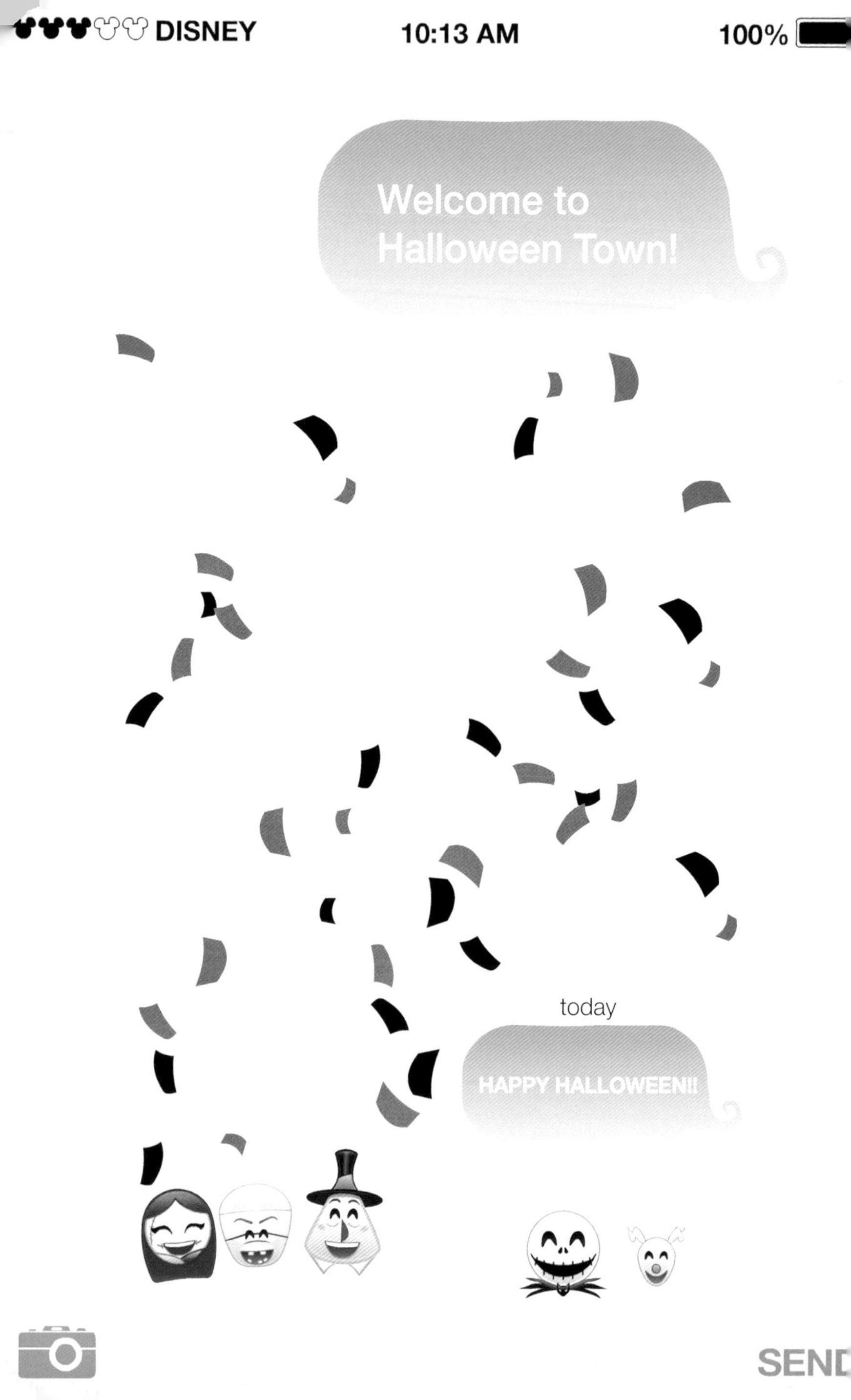
DISNEY
10:13 AM
100%
Welcome to Halloween Town!
today
HAPPY HALLOWEEN!!
SEND

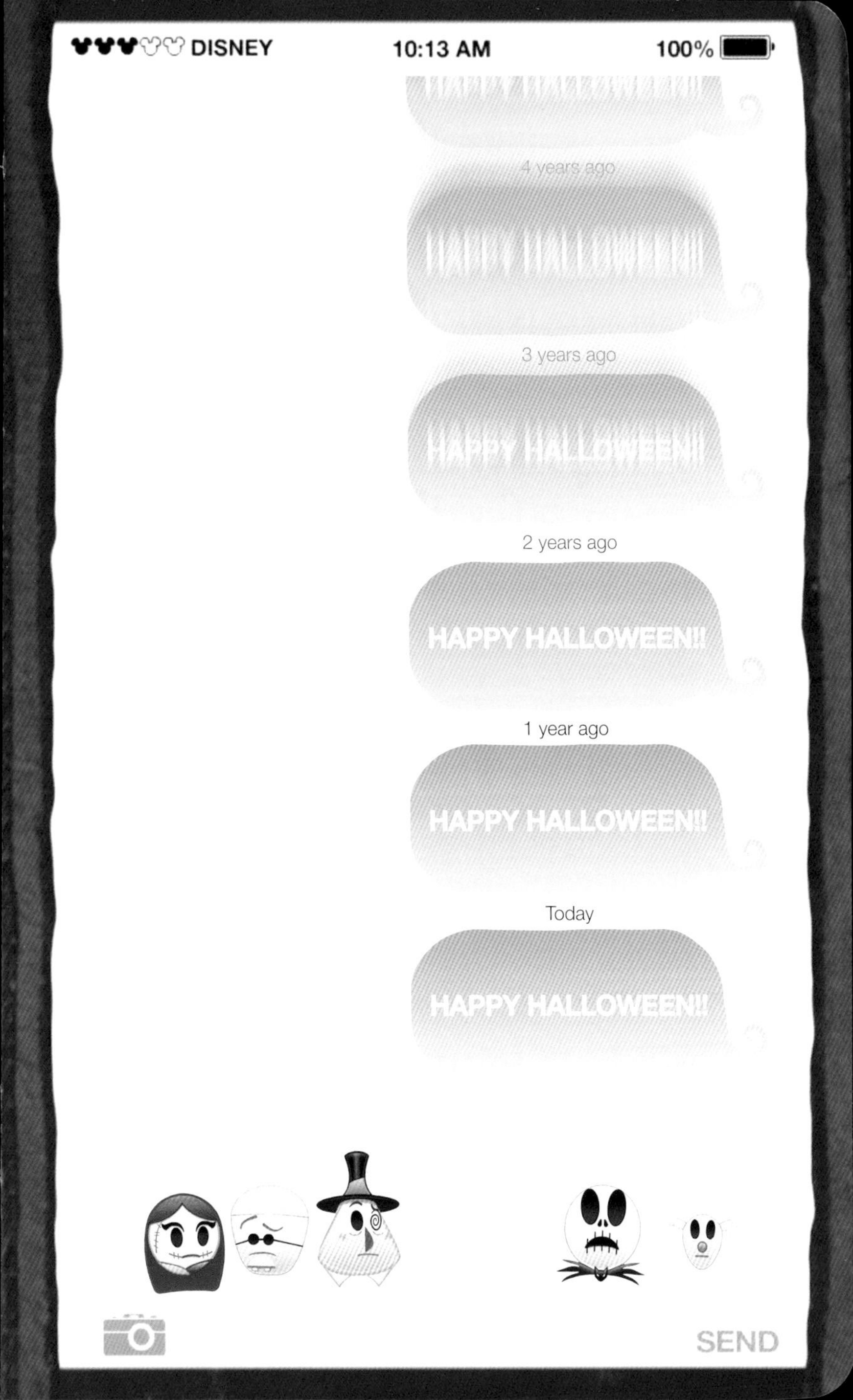
DISNEY
10:13 AM
100%
4 years ago
HAPPY HALLOWEEN!!
3 years ago
HAPPY HALLOWEEN!!
2 years ago
HAPPY HALLOWEEN!!
1 year ago
HAPPY HALLOWEEN!!
Today
HAPPY HALLOWEEN!!
SEND

100 years ago

HAPPY HALLOWEEN!!

50 years ago

HAPPY HALLOWEEN!!

10 years ago

HAPPY HALLOWEEN!!

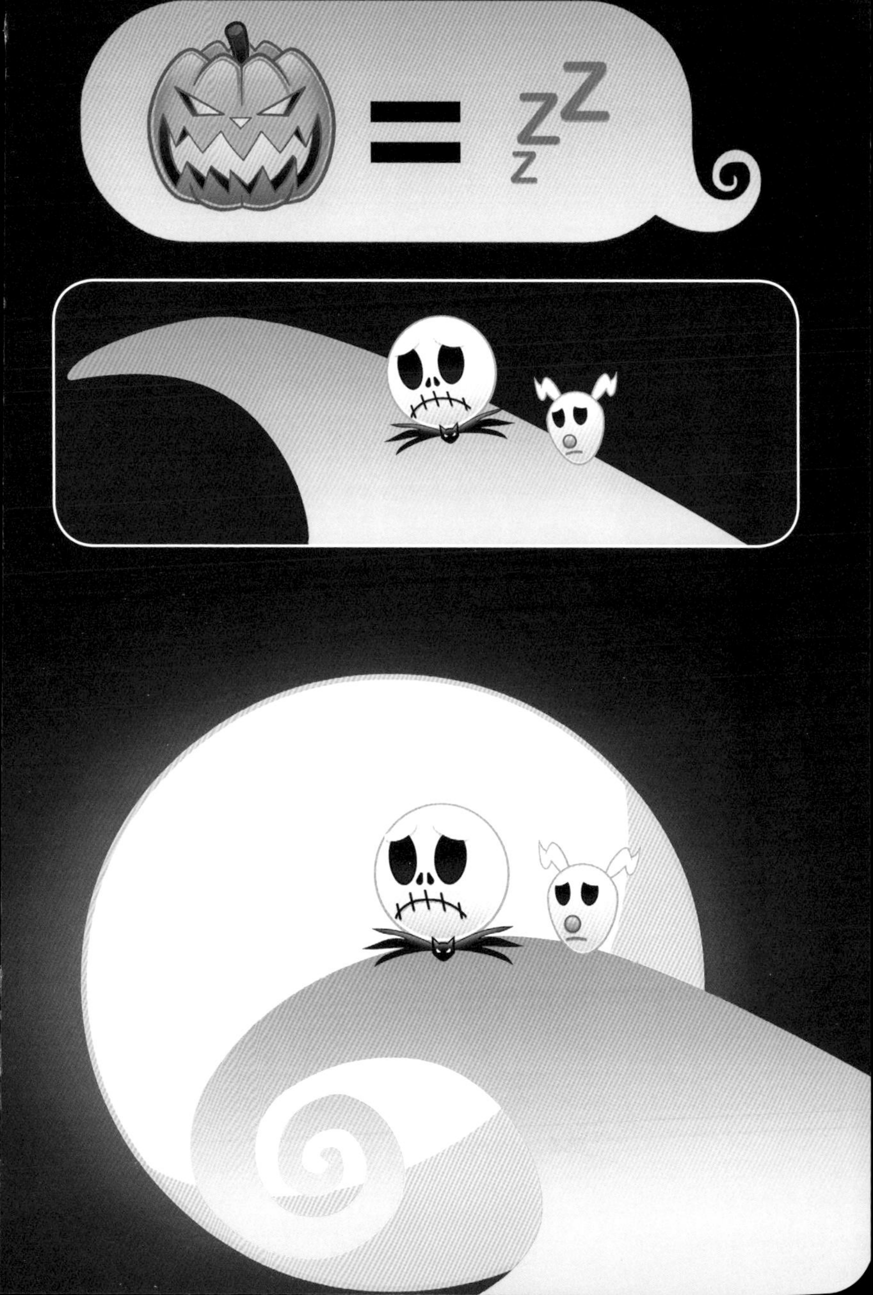

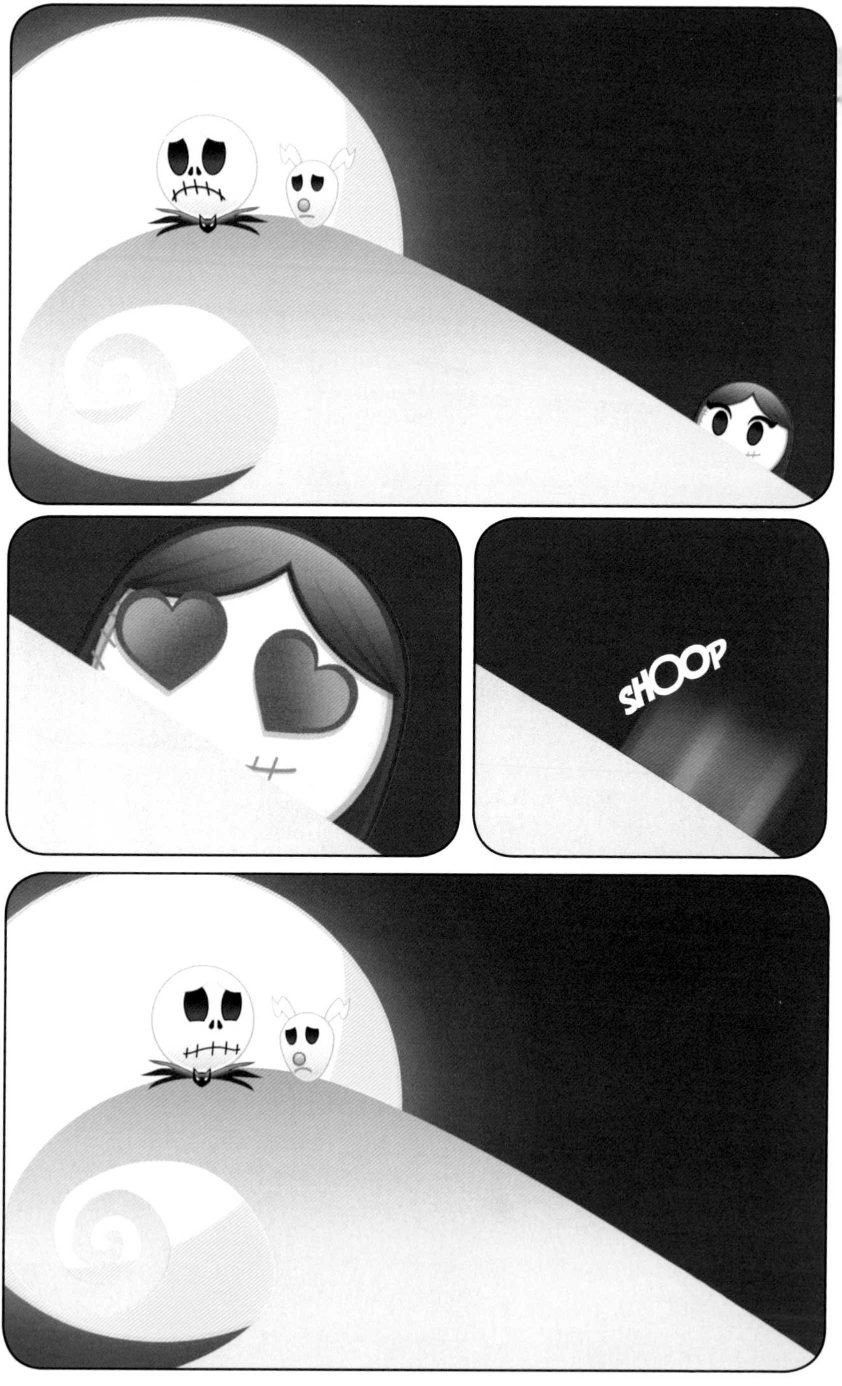
SHOOP

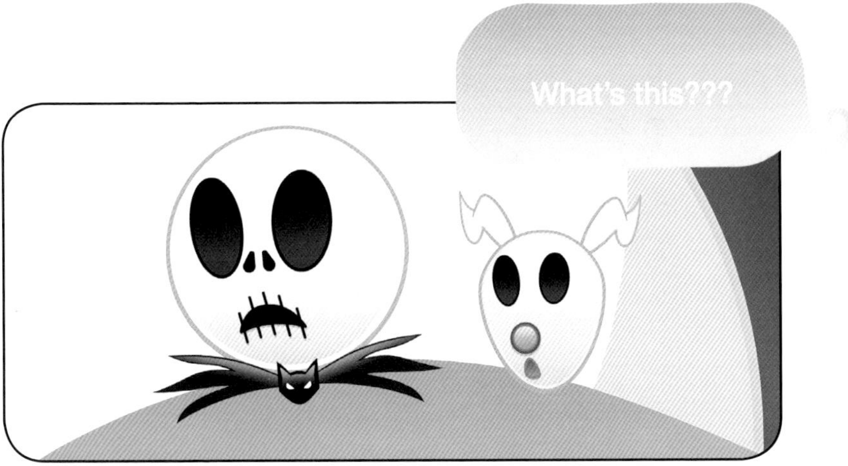
What's this???

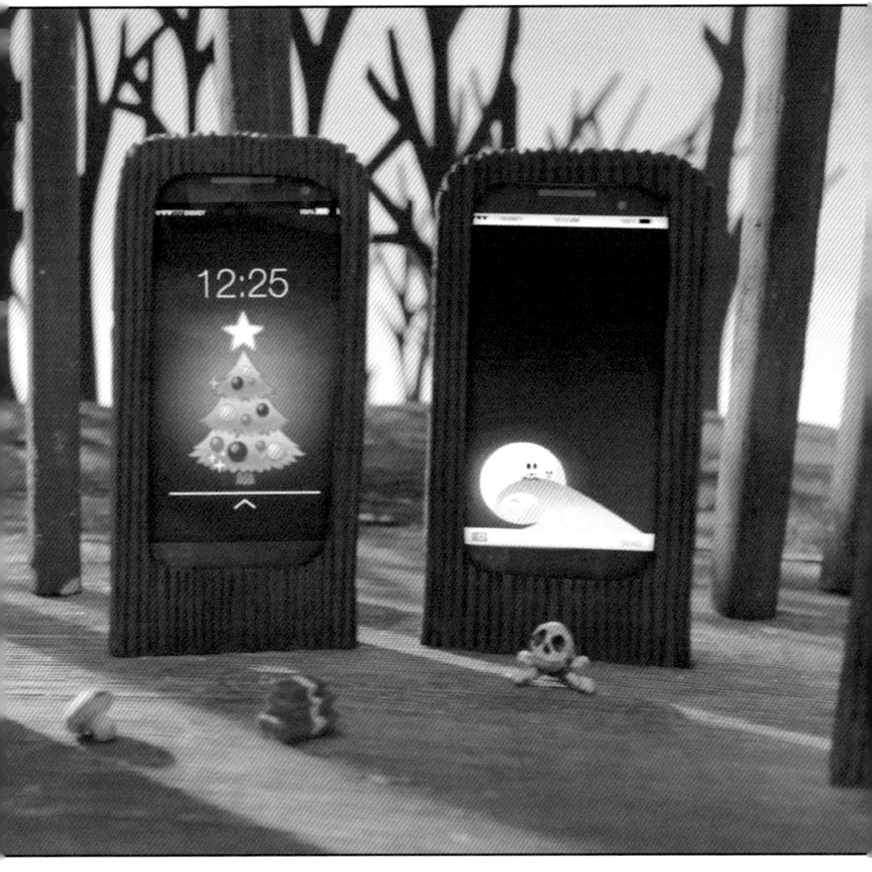
12:25

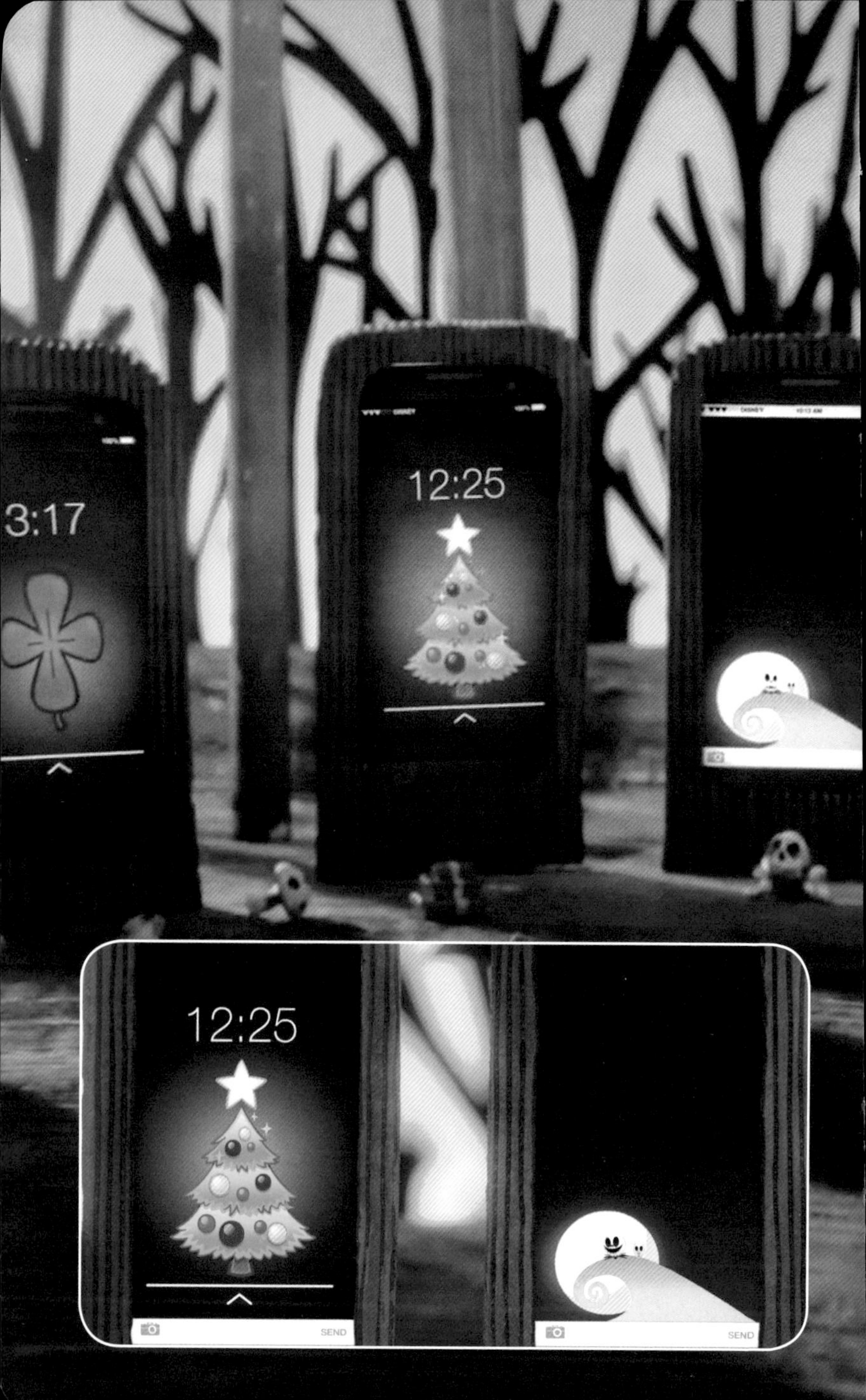
3:17
12:25
12:25
SEND
SEND

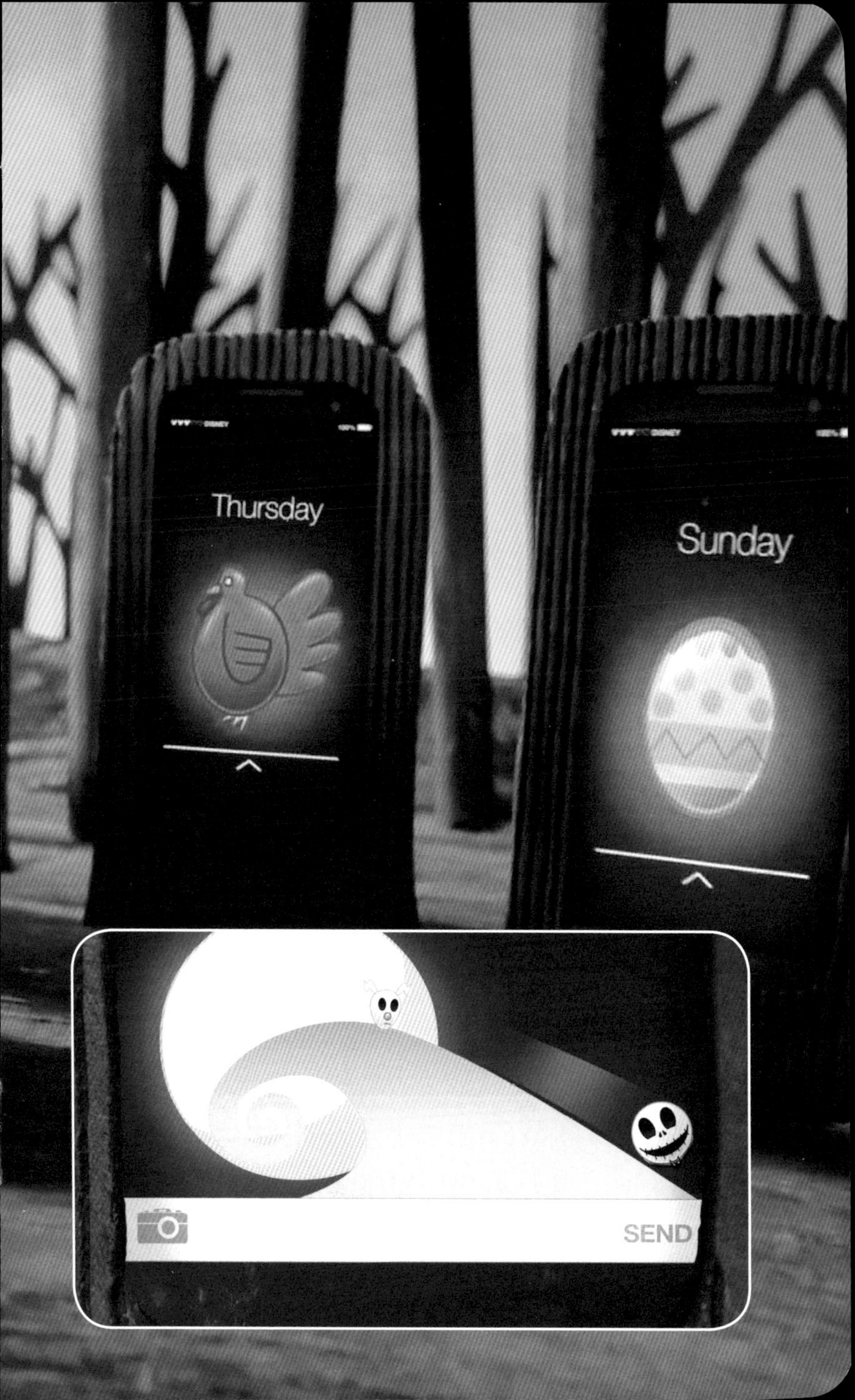

Thursday
Sunday
SEND

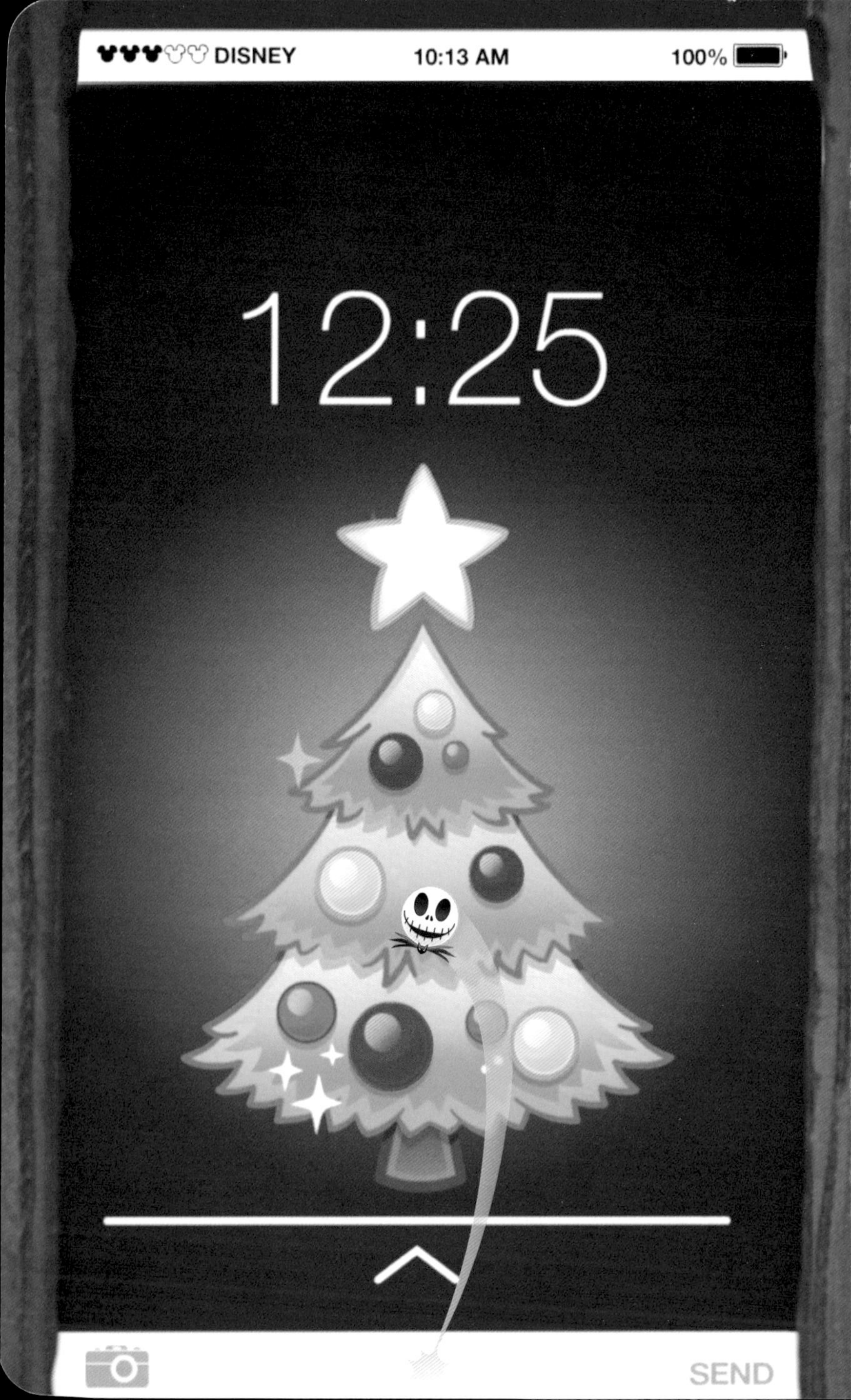
DISNEY
10:13 AM
100%
12:25
SEND

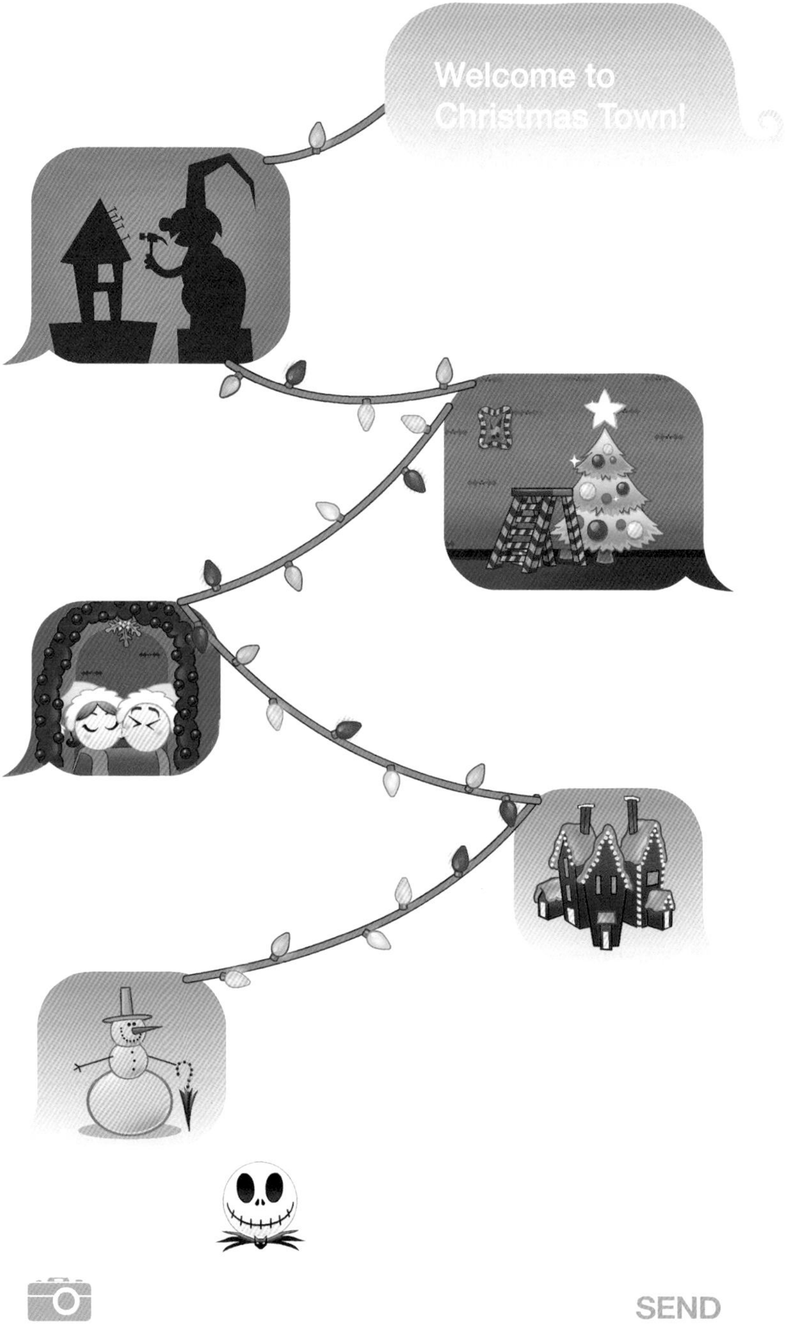
Welcome to
Christmas Town!
SEND

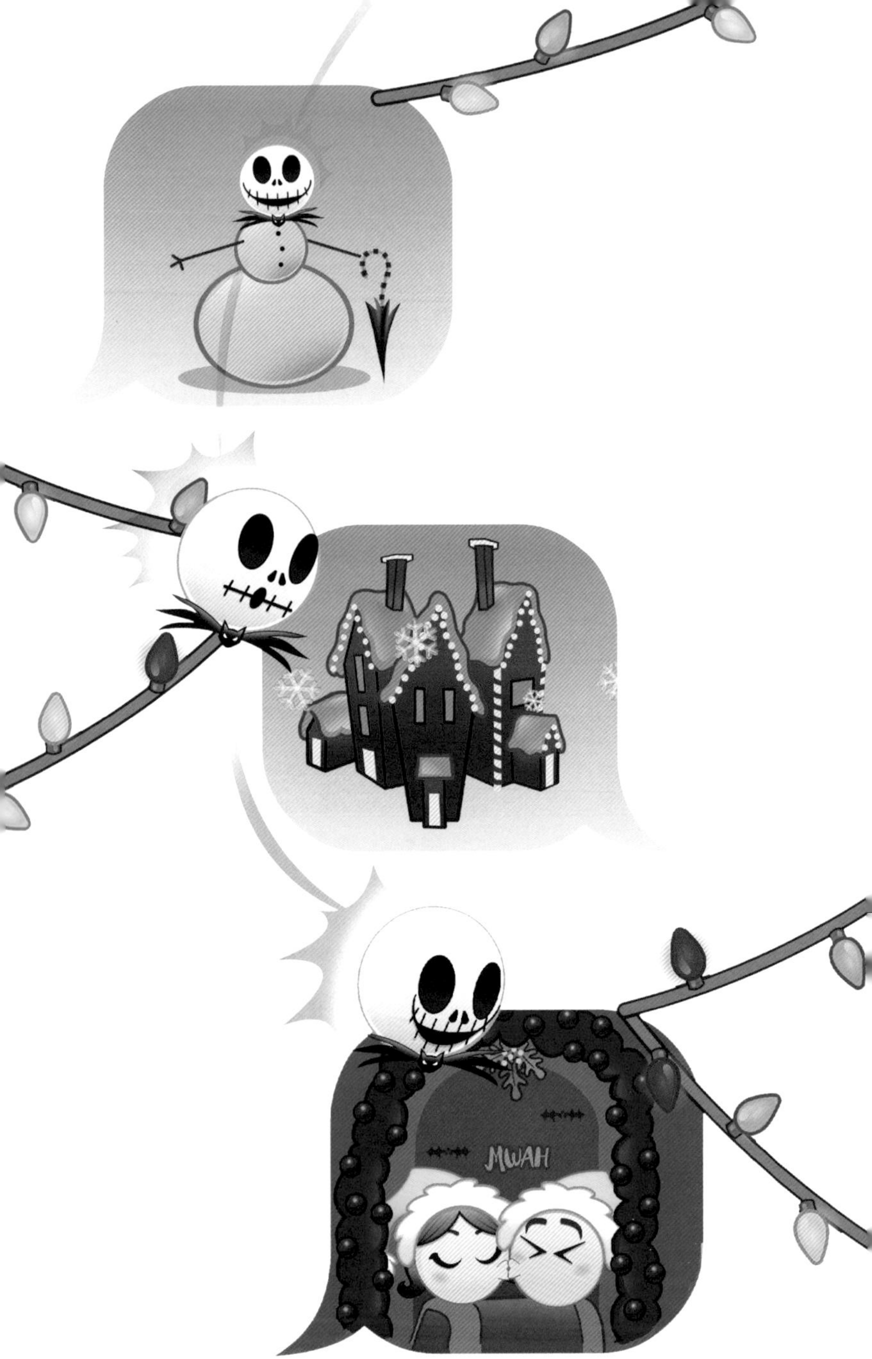
MWAH

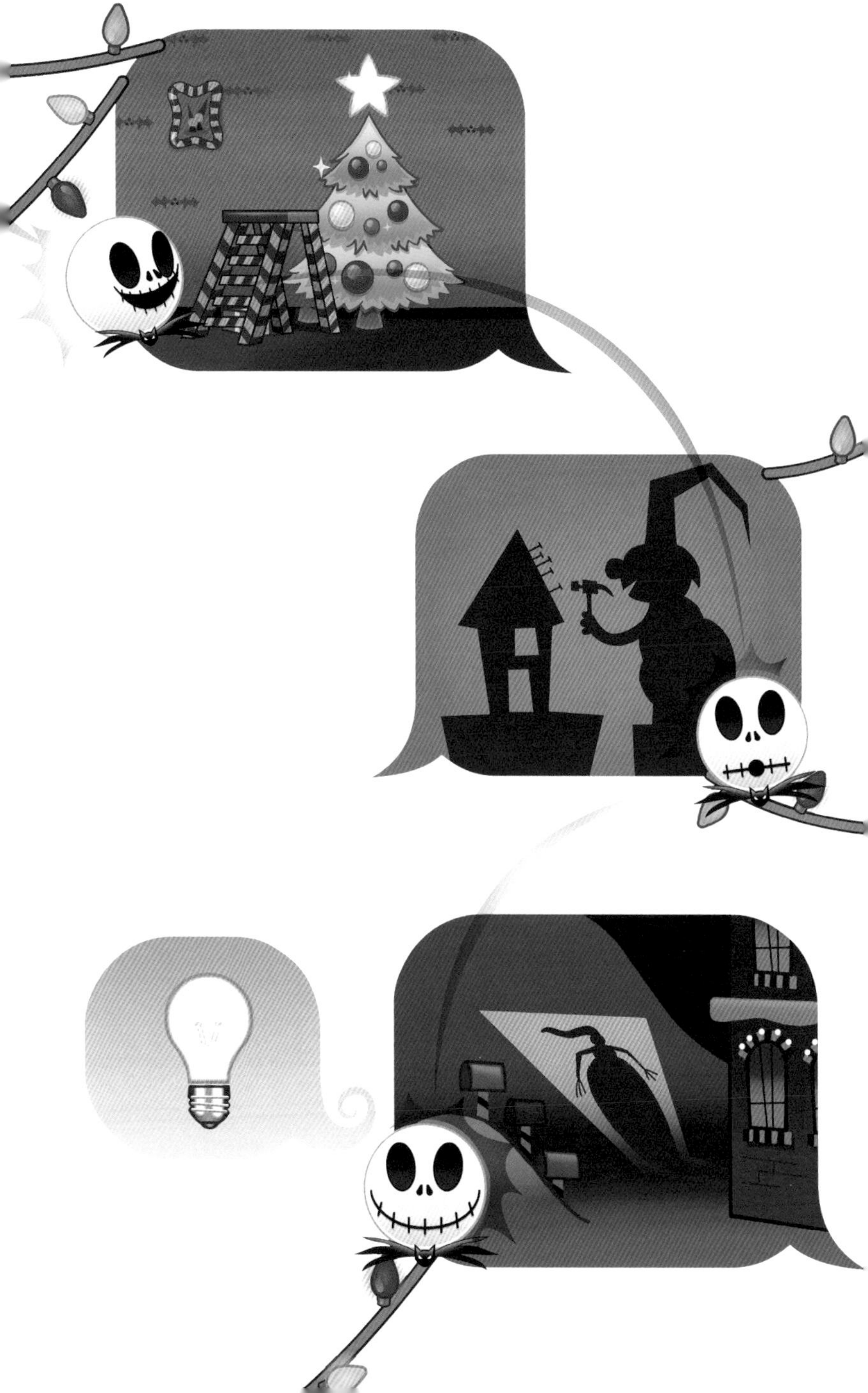

Meanwhile...

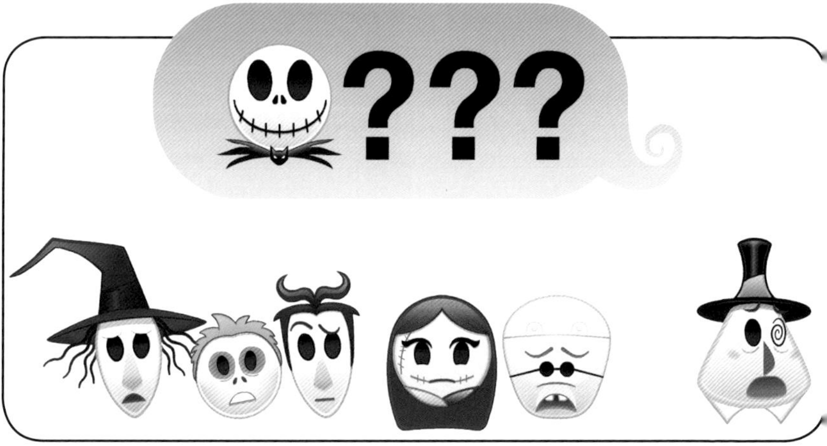
???

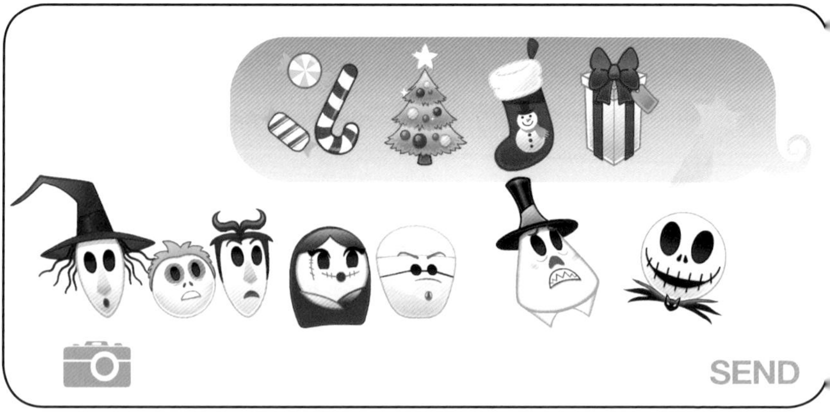
SEND

DEC
25

calendar

SEND

Jack and the rest of Halloween Town decide to take over Christmas this year!

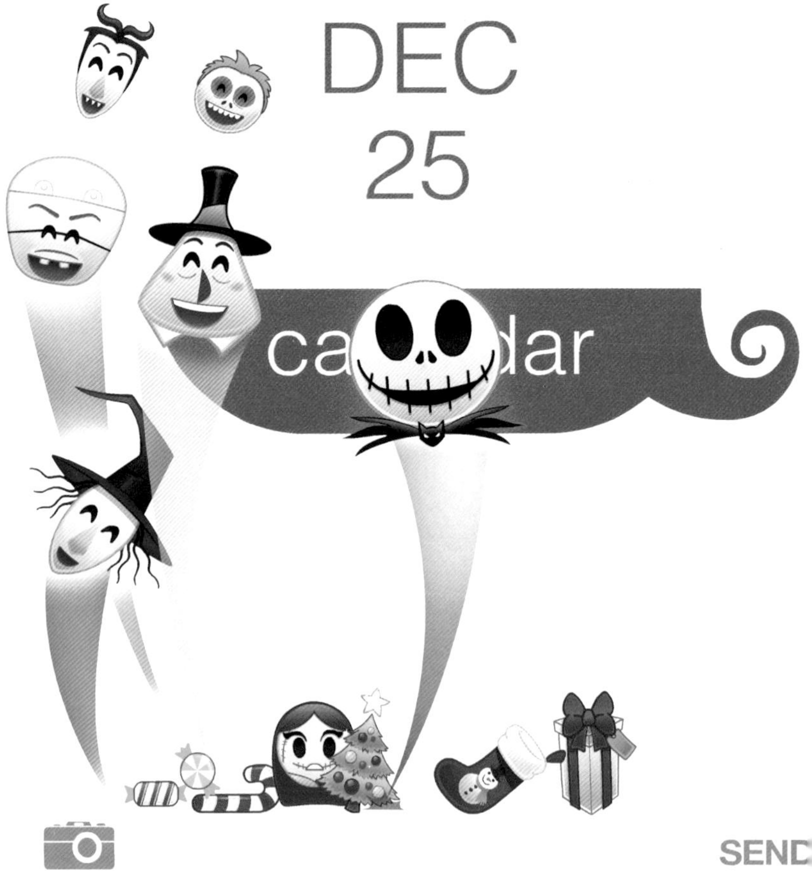
DEC
25
ca
dar
SEND

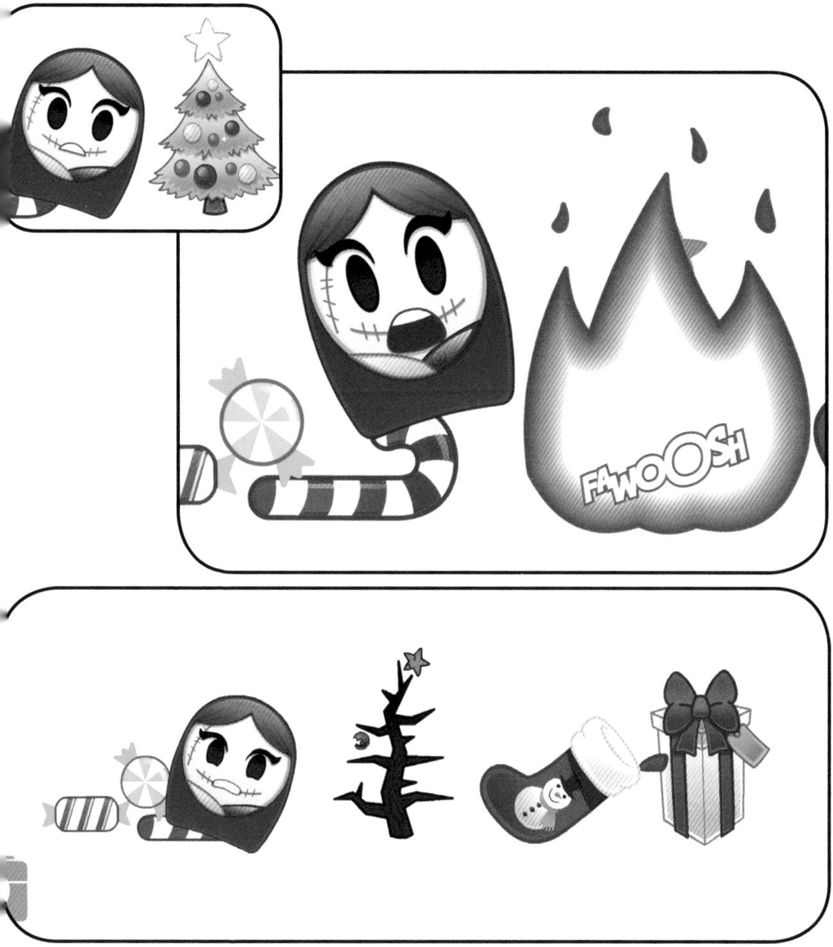
FAWOOSH

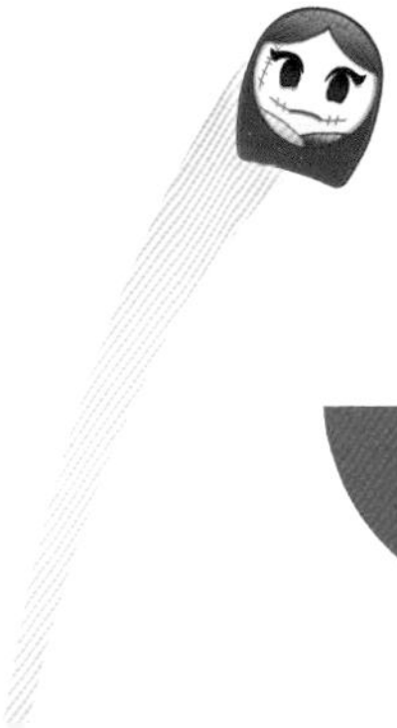

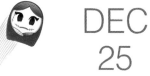

DEC
25

calendar

≡ Q +

November

Nov 9

Nov 10

Nov 11

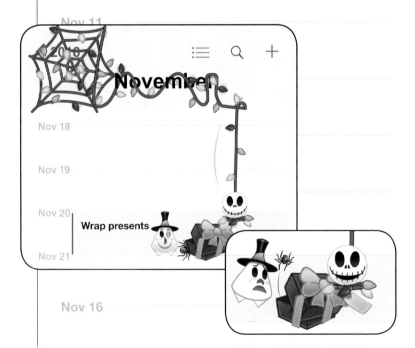

≡ Q +

November

Nov 18

Nov 19

Nov 20

Wrap presents

Nov 21

Nov 16

Today   **Calendars**   **Inbox**

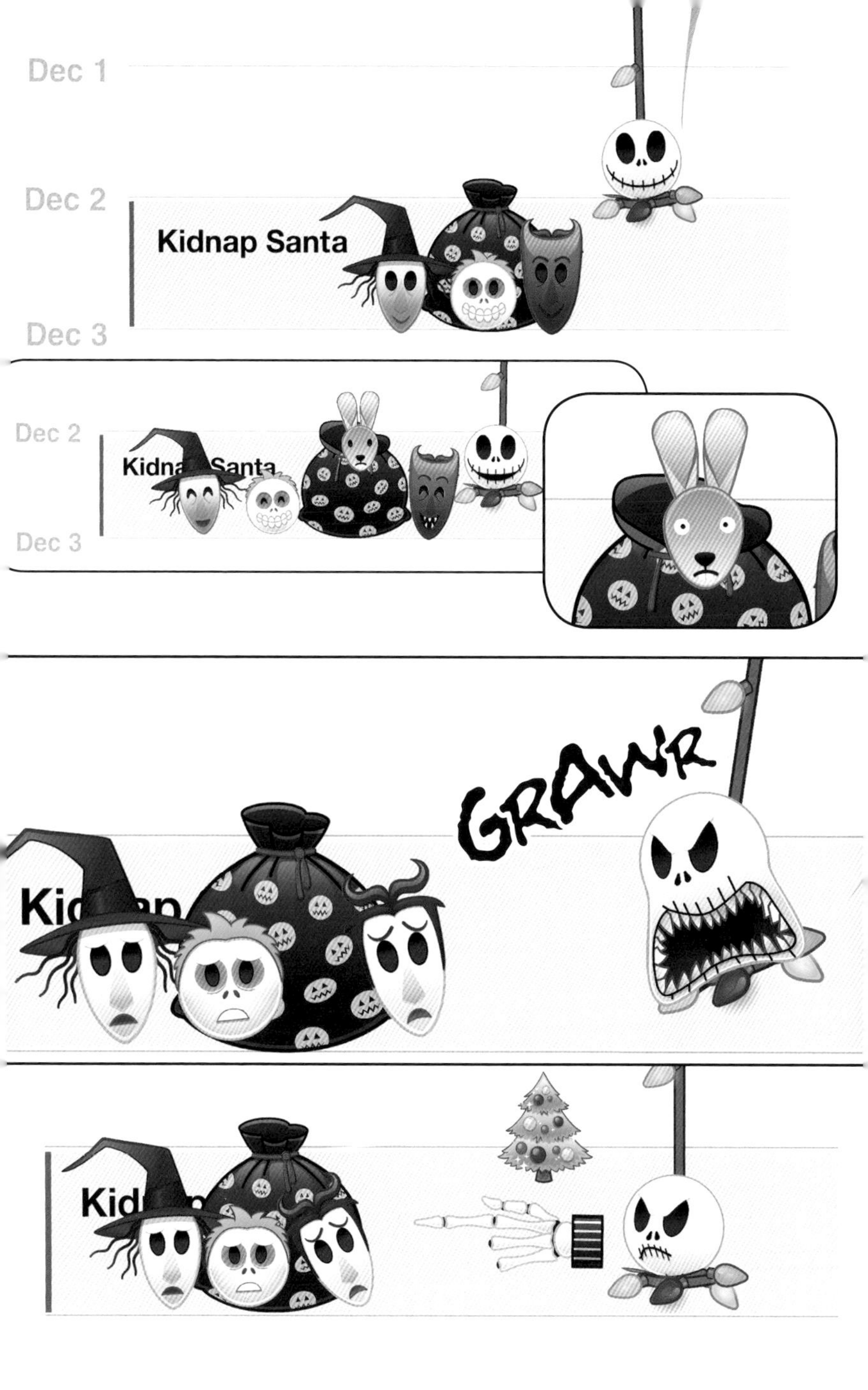
Dec 1
Dec 2
Kidnap Santa
Dec 3
Dec 2
Kidnap Santa
Dec 3
GRAWR

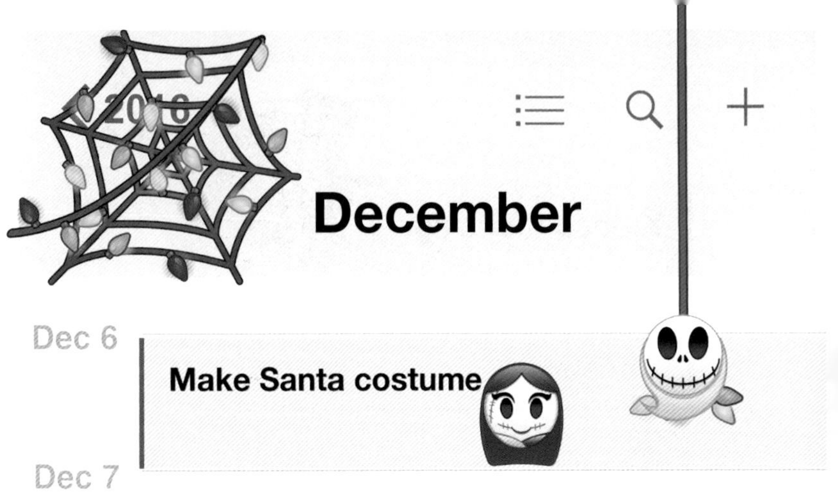
December
Dec 6
Make Santa costume
Dec 7

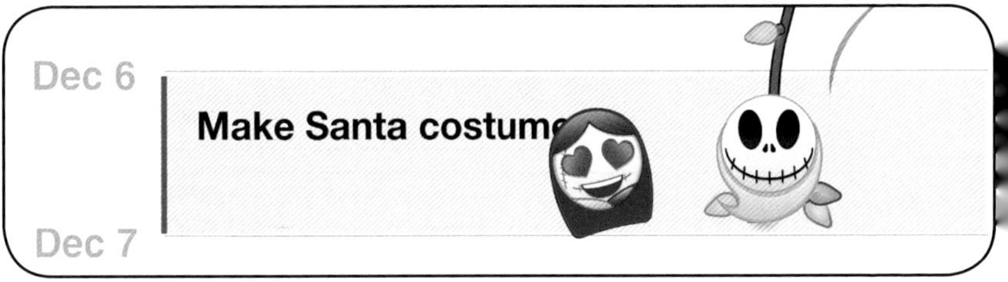
Dec 6
Make Santa costume
Dec 7

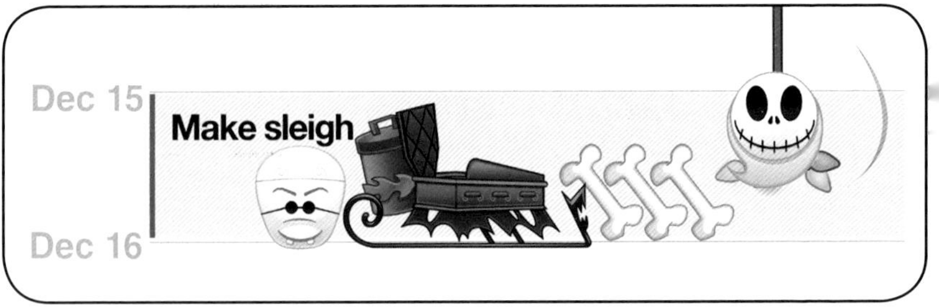
Dec 15
Make sleigh
Dec 16

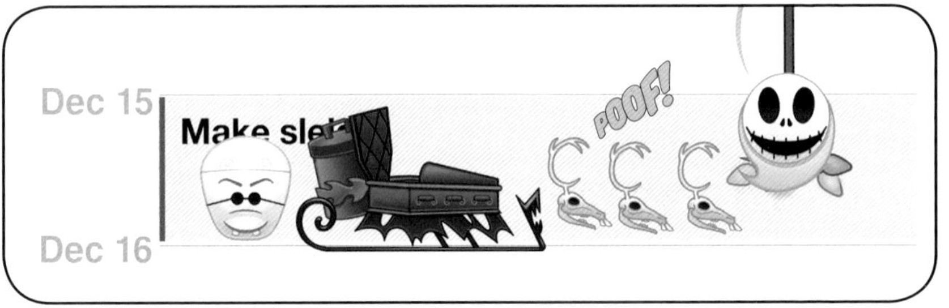
Dec 15
POOF!
Dec 16

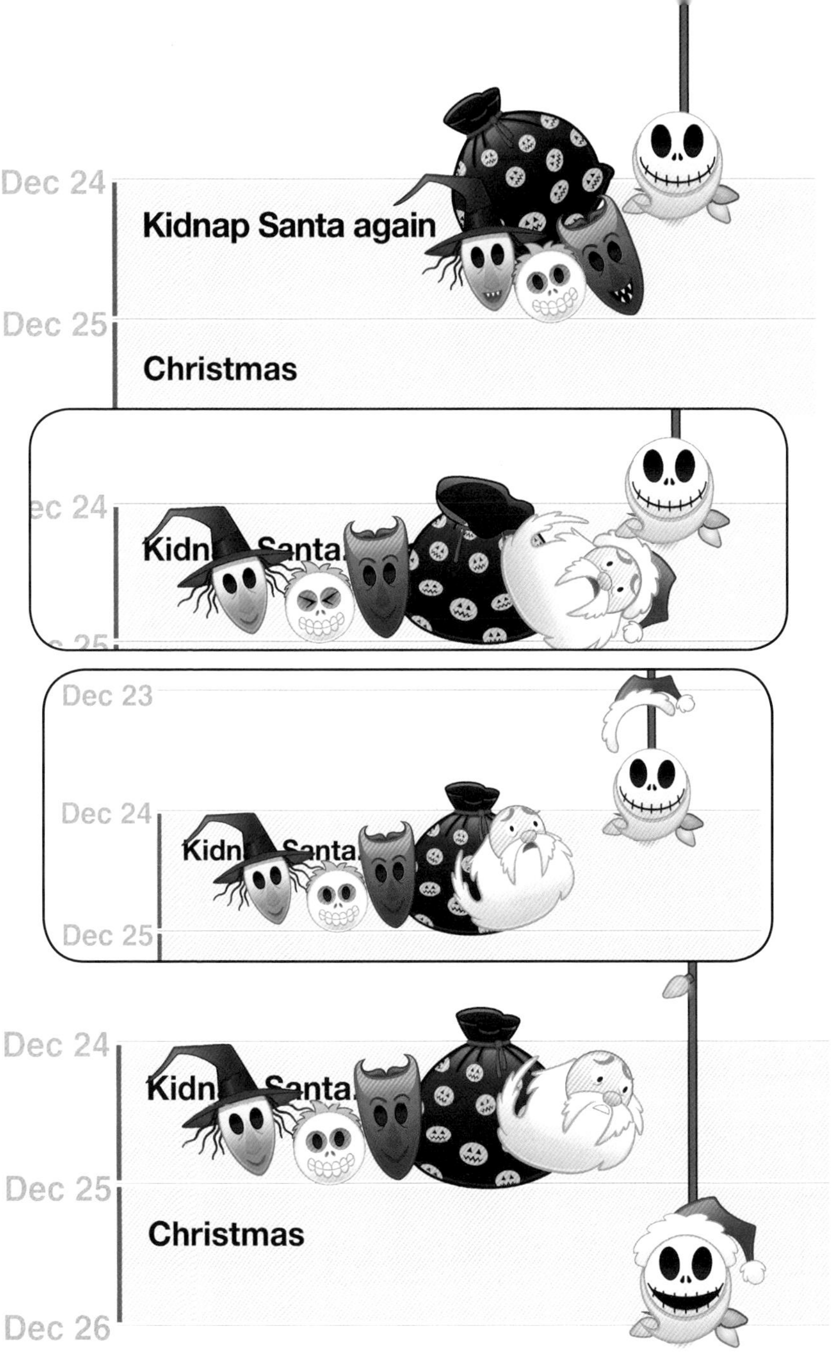
Dec 24
Kidnap Santa again
Dec 25
Christmas
Dec 23
Dec 24
Dec 25
Dec 24
Dec 25
Christmas
Dec 26

Dec 22

Dec 23

FWING

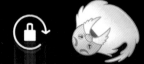 

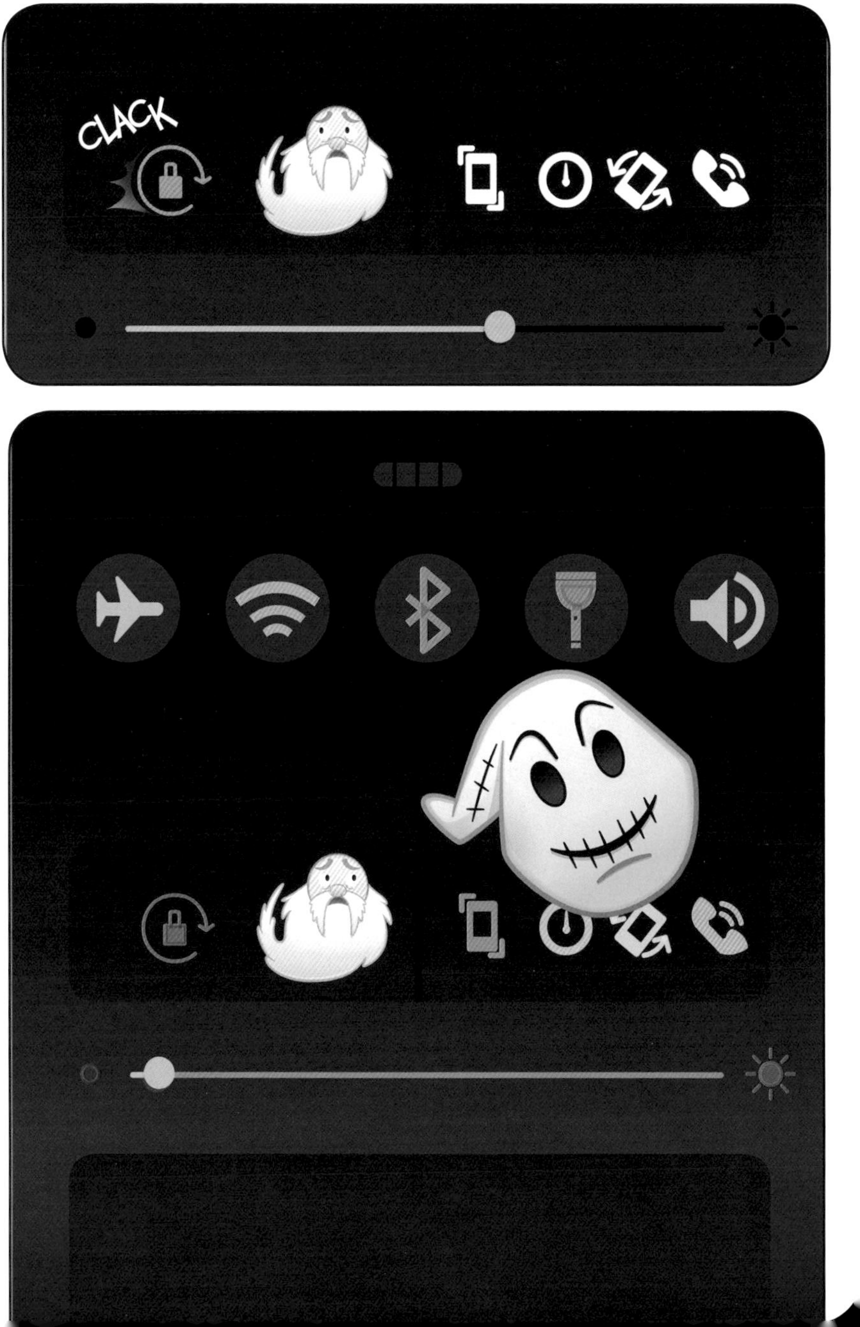
CLACK

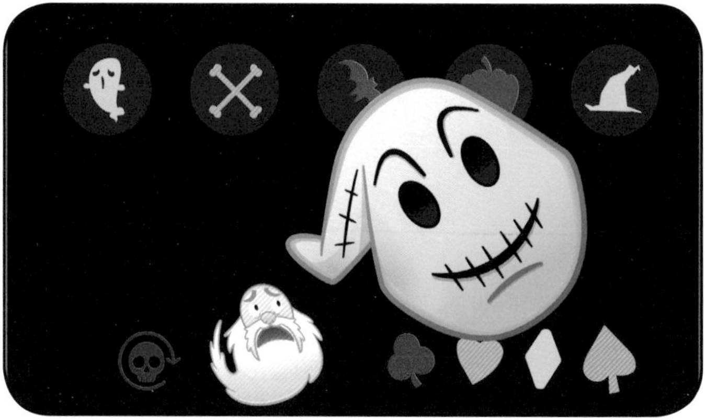

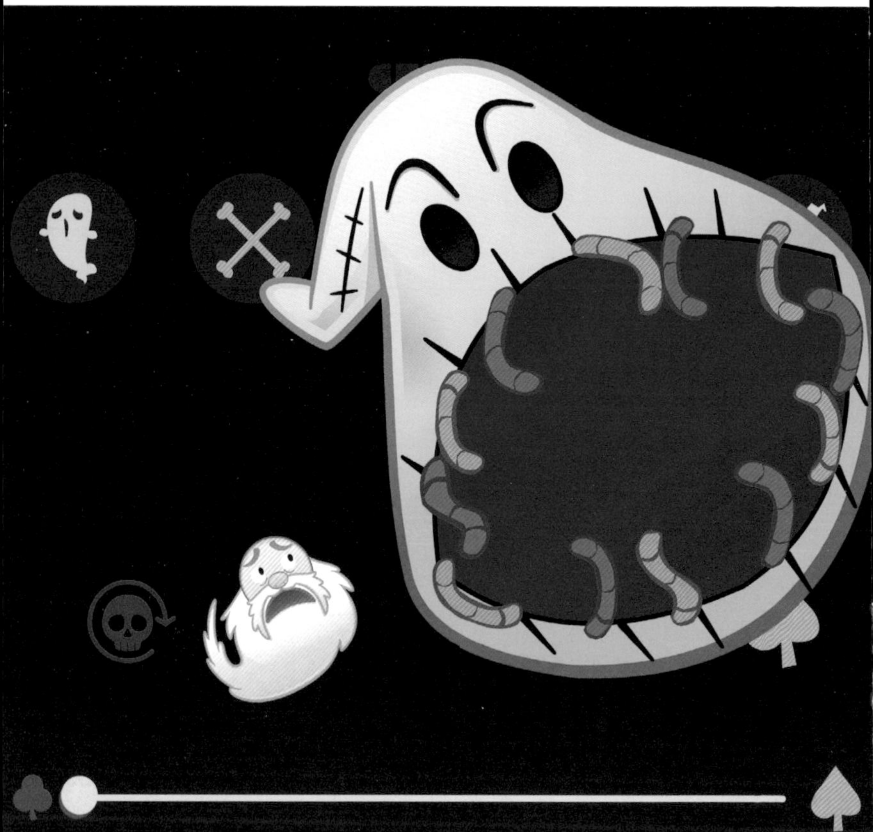

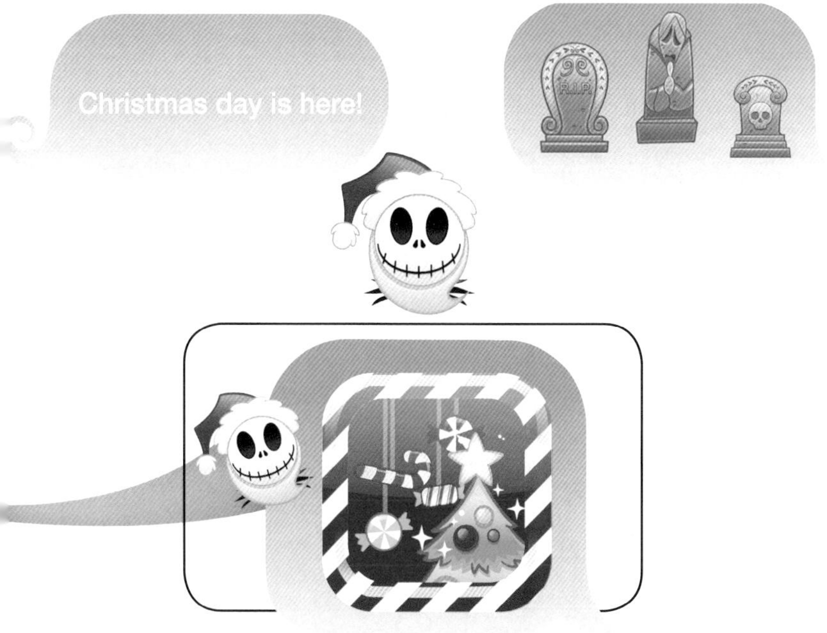
Christmas day is here!

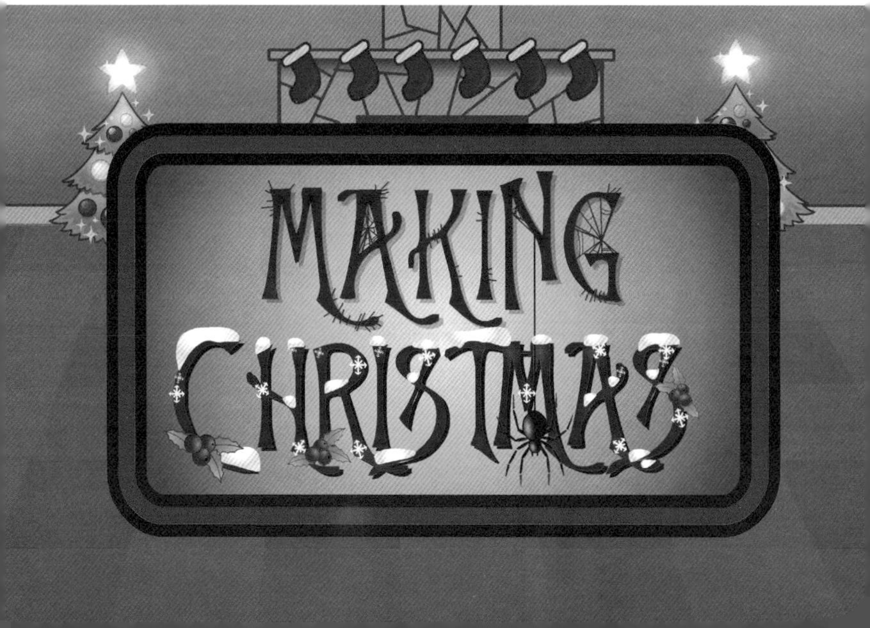
MAKING
CHRISTMAS

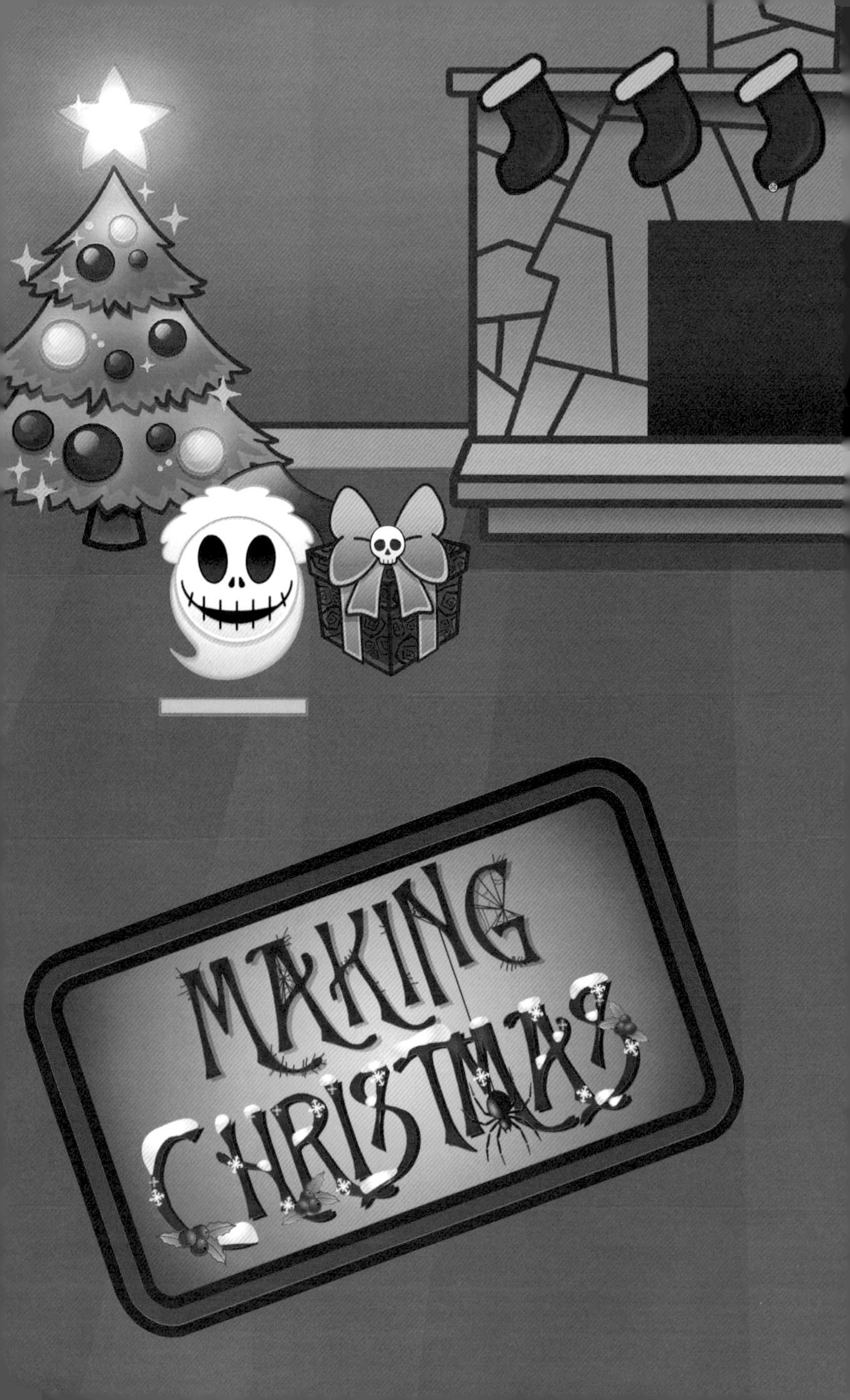
MAKING CHRISTMAS

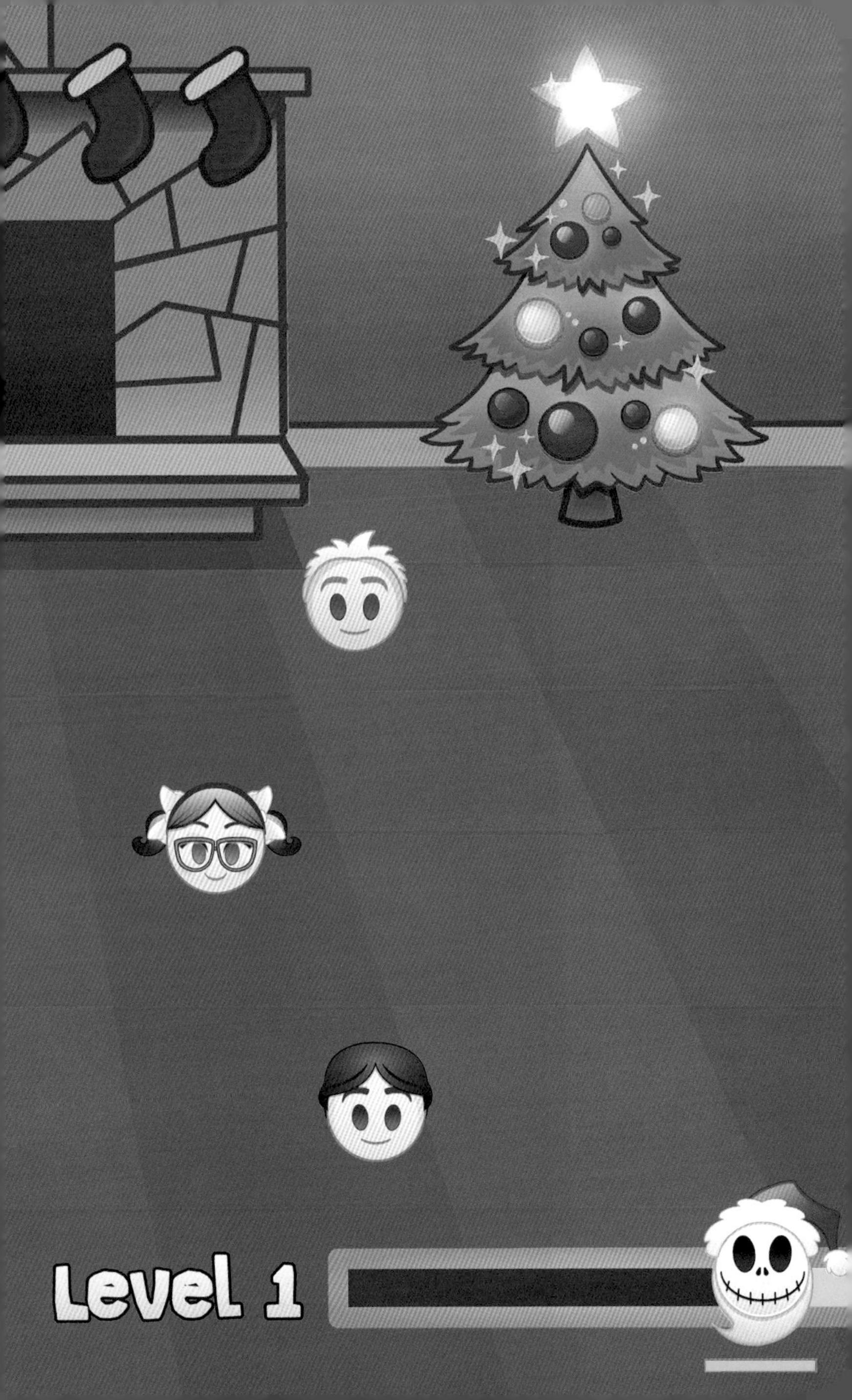
Level 1

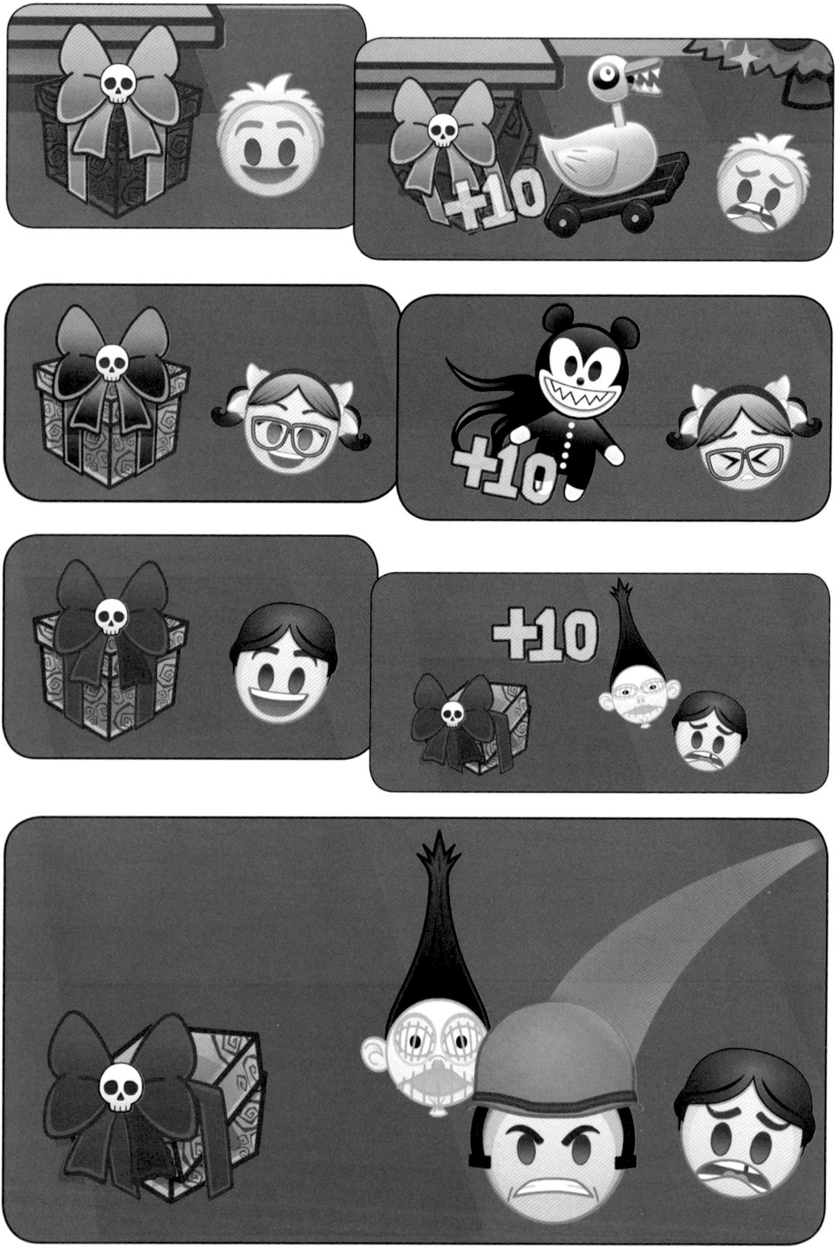
+10
+10
+10

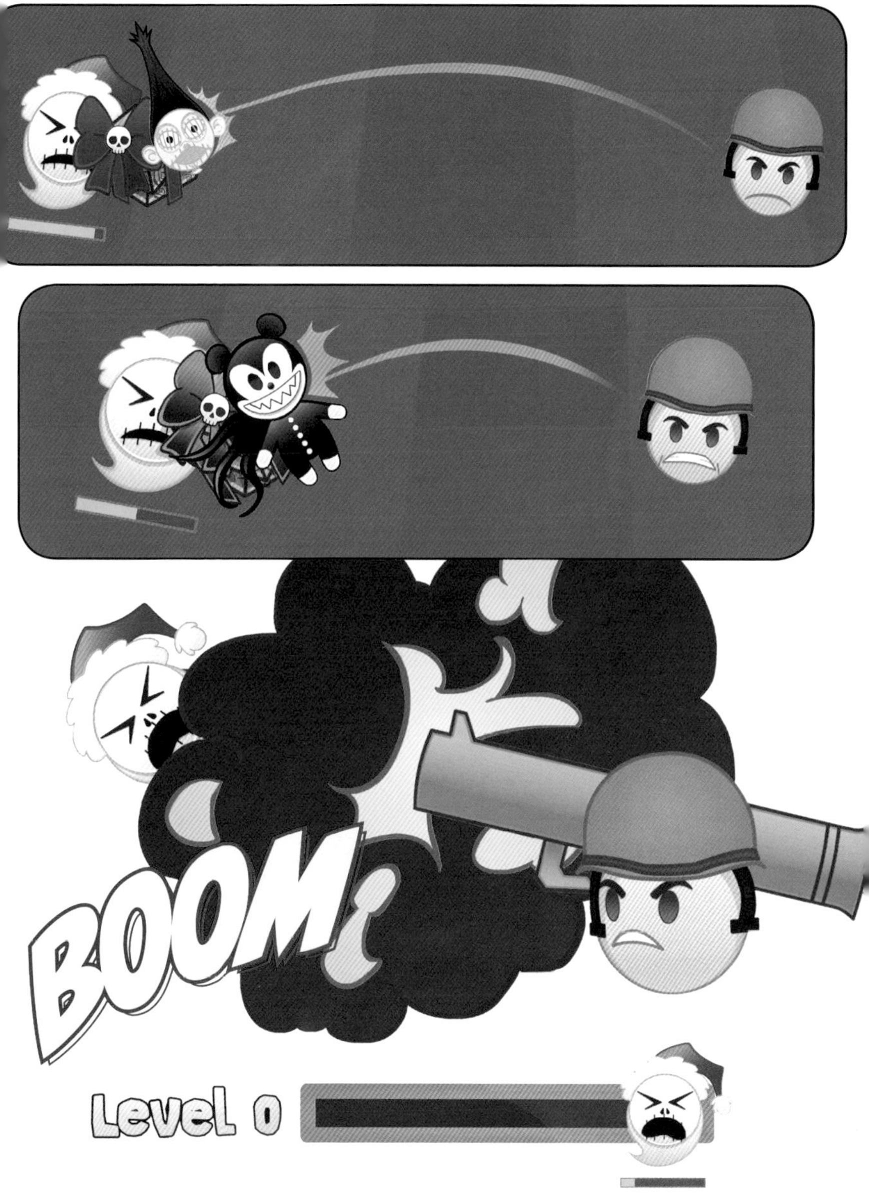
BOOM!
Level 0

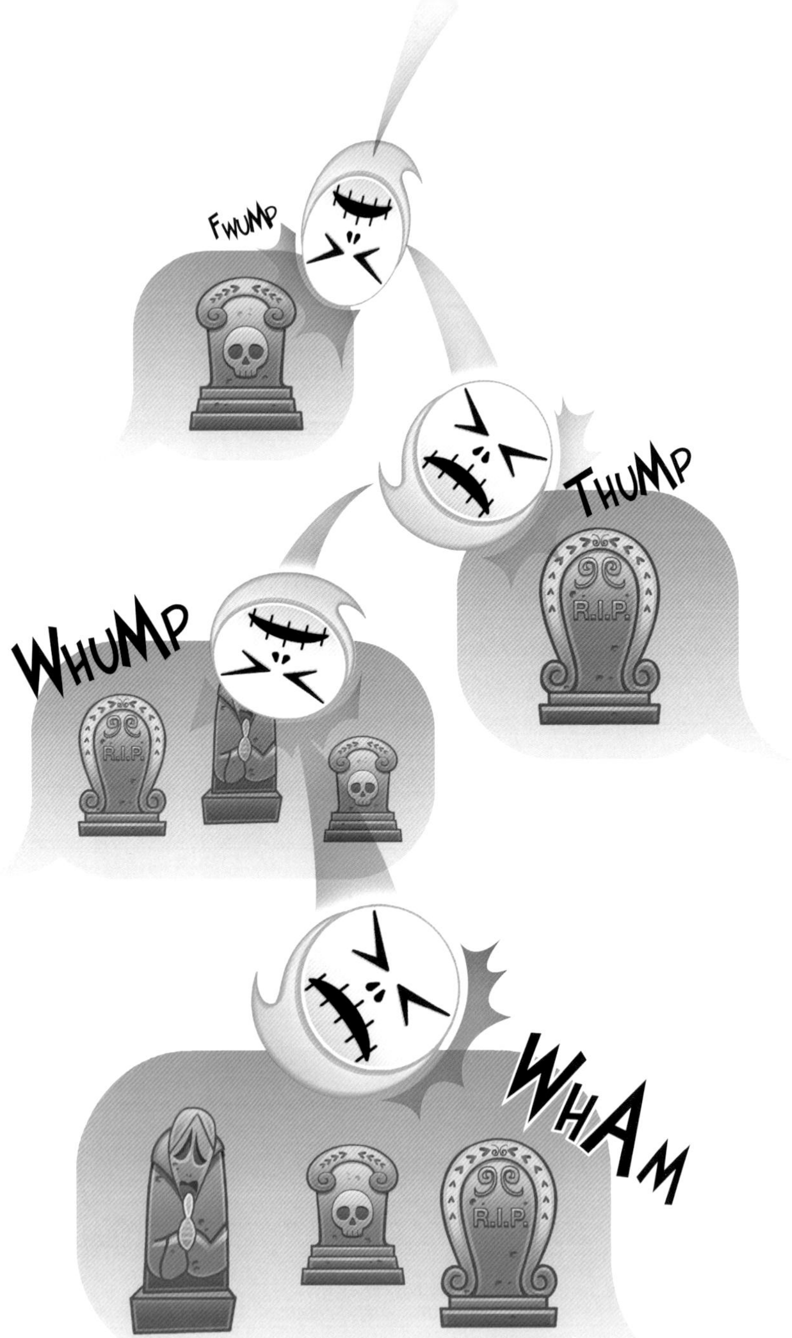
FWUMP
THUMP
WHUMP
WHAM

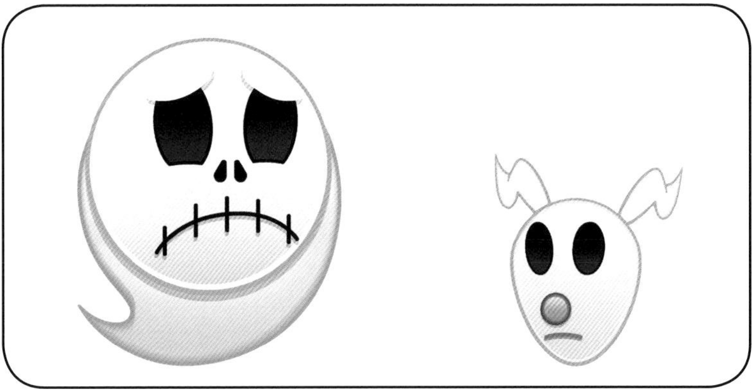

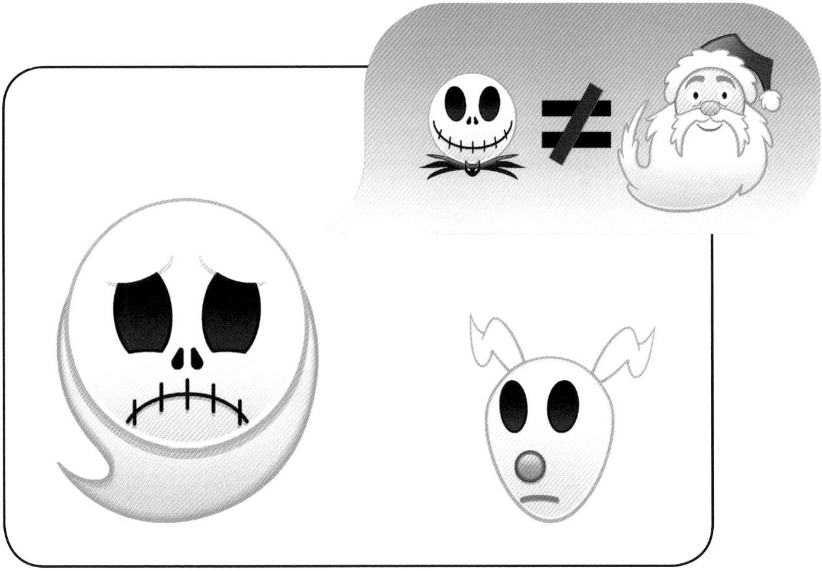

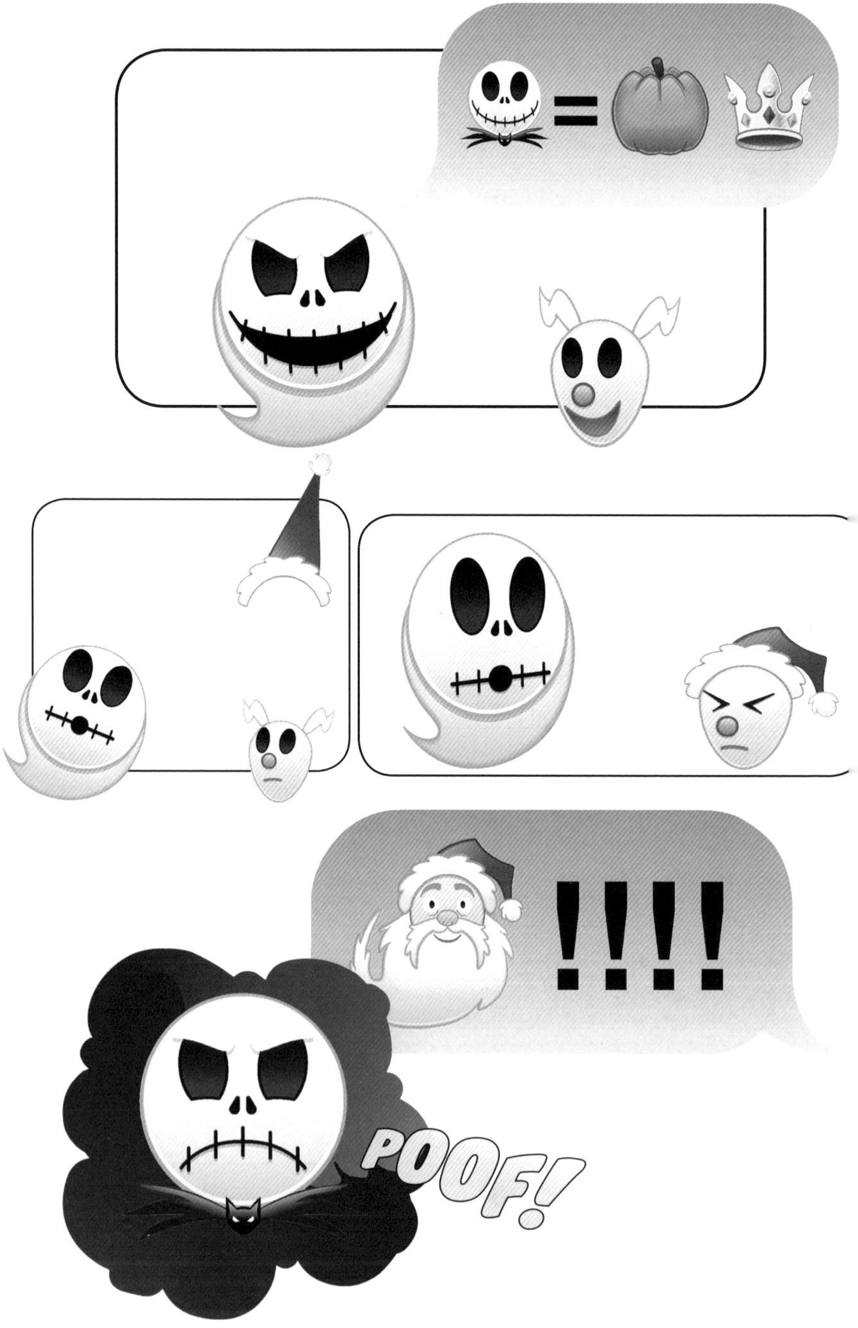
!!!!
POOF!

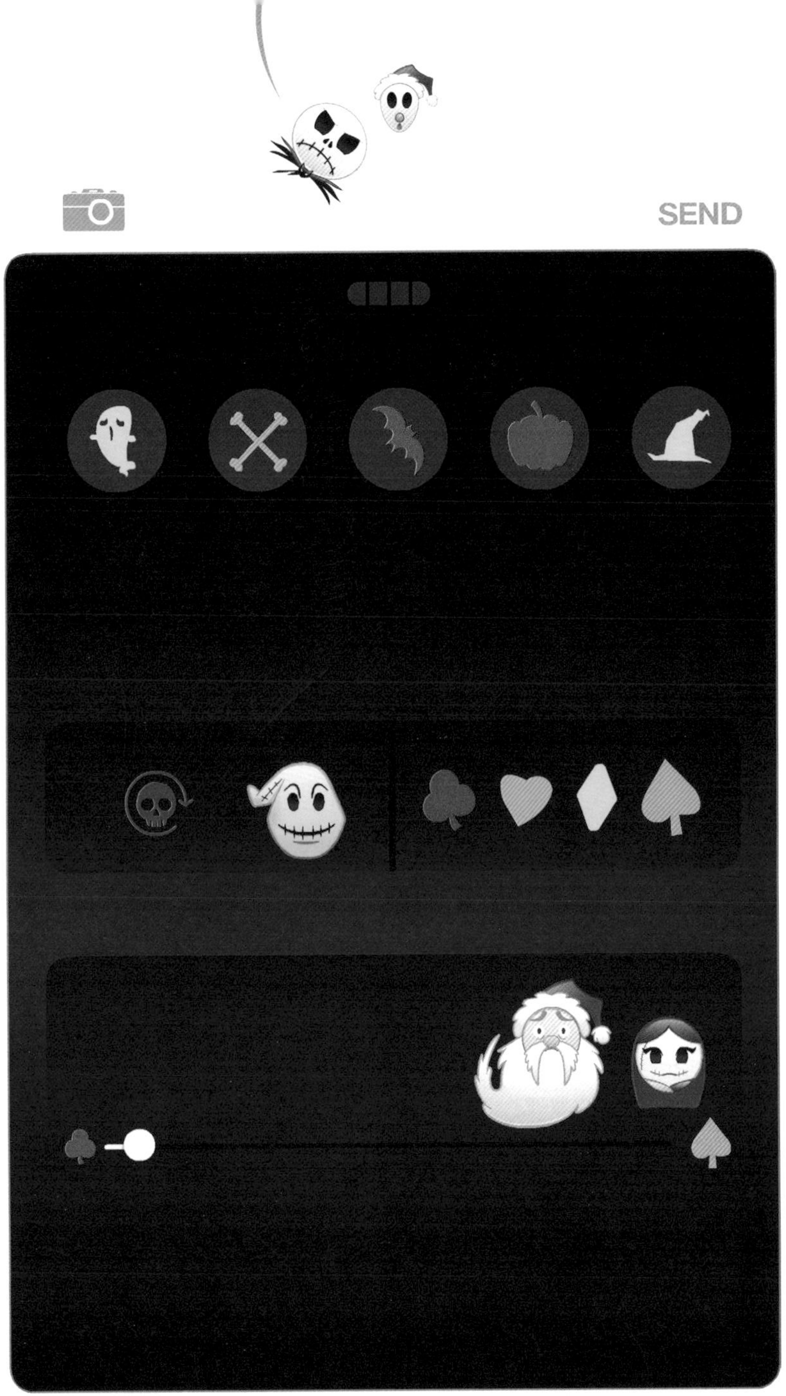
SEND

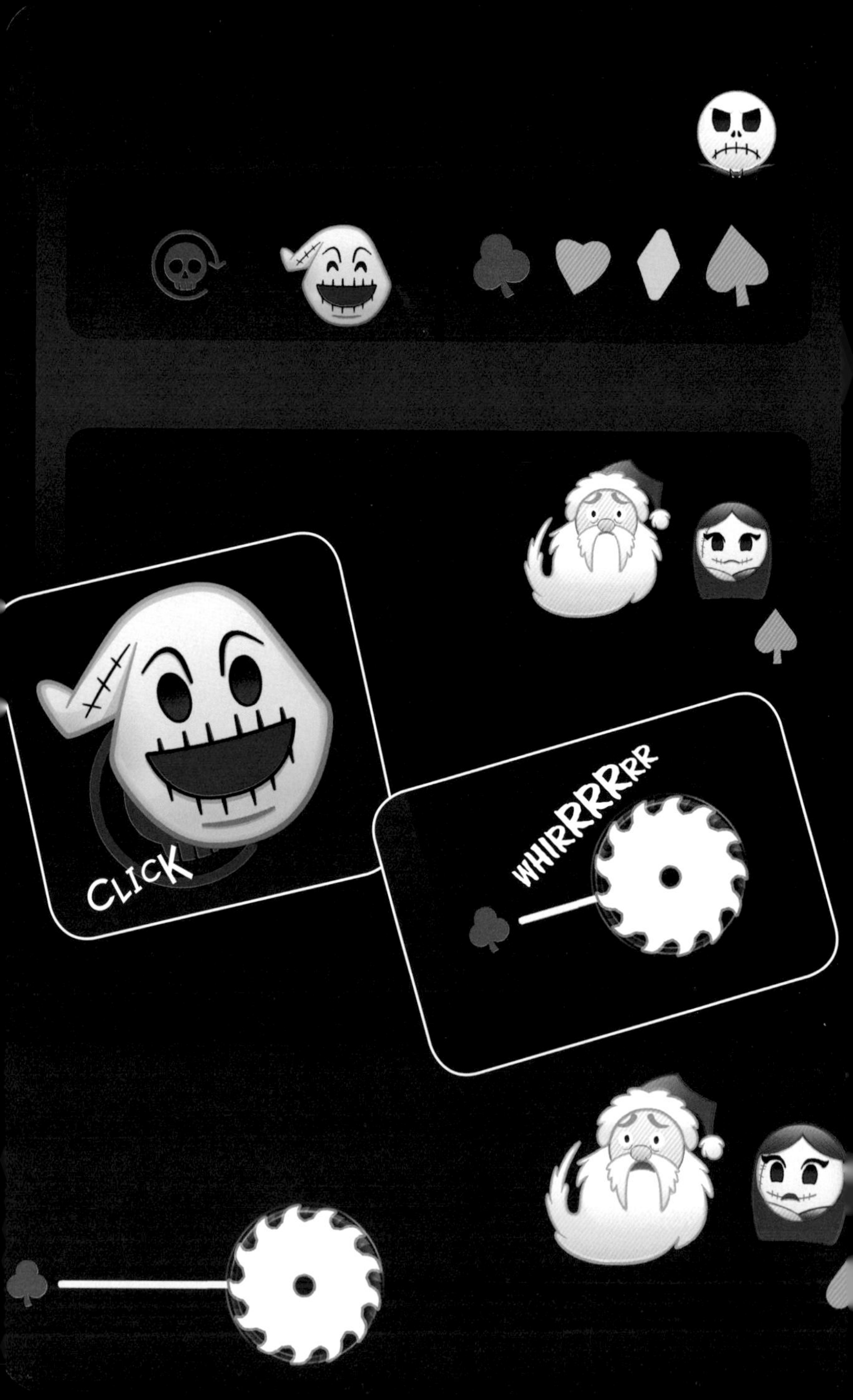
CLICK
WHIRRRRRR

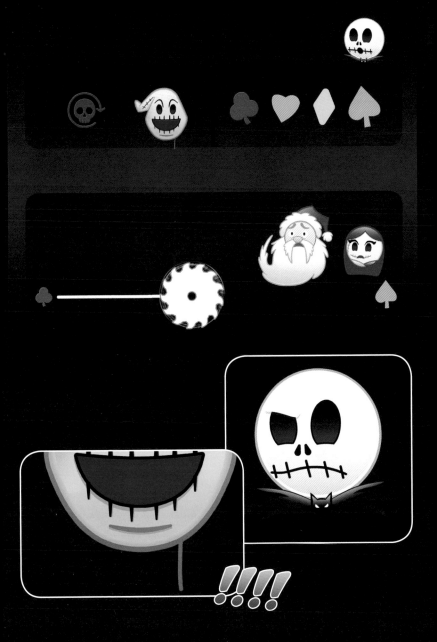

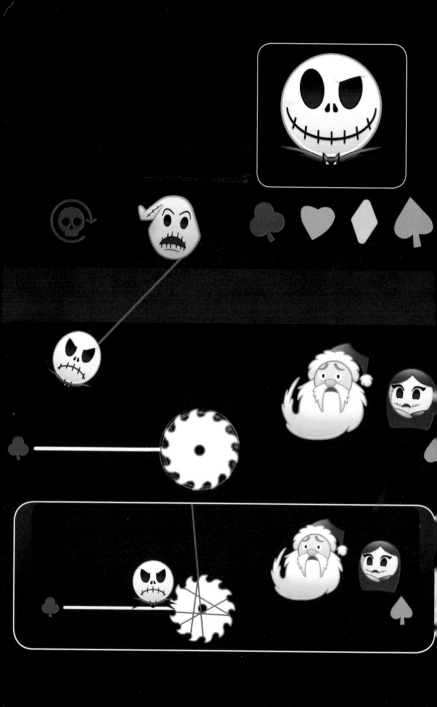

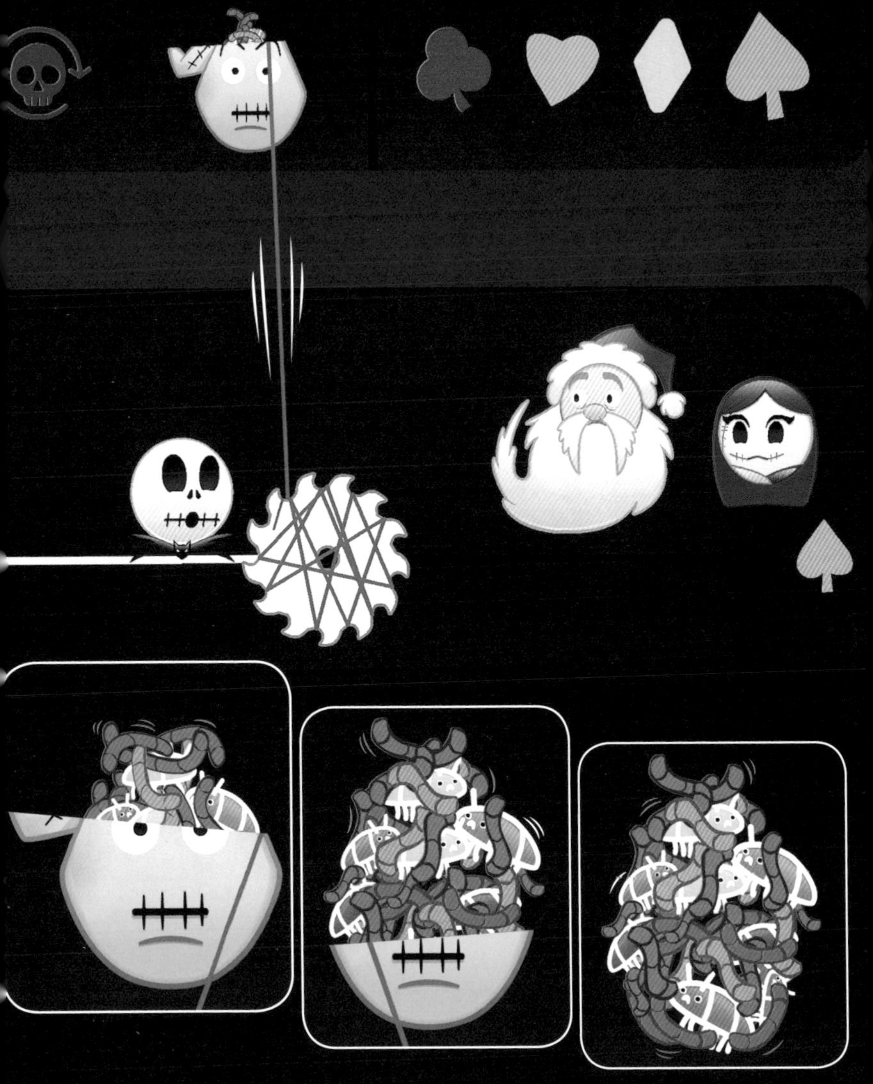

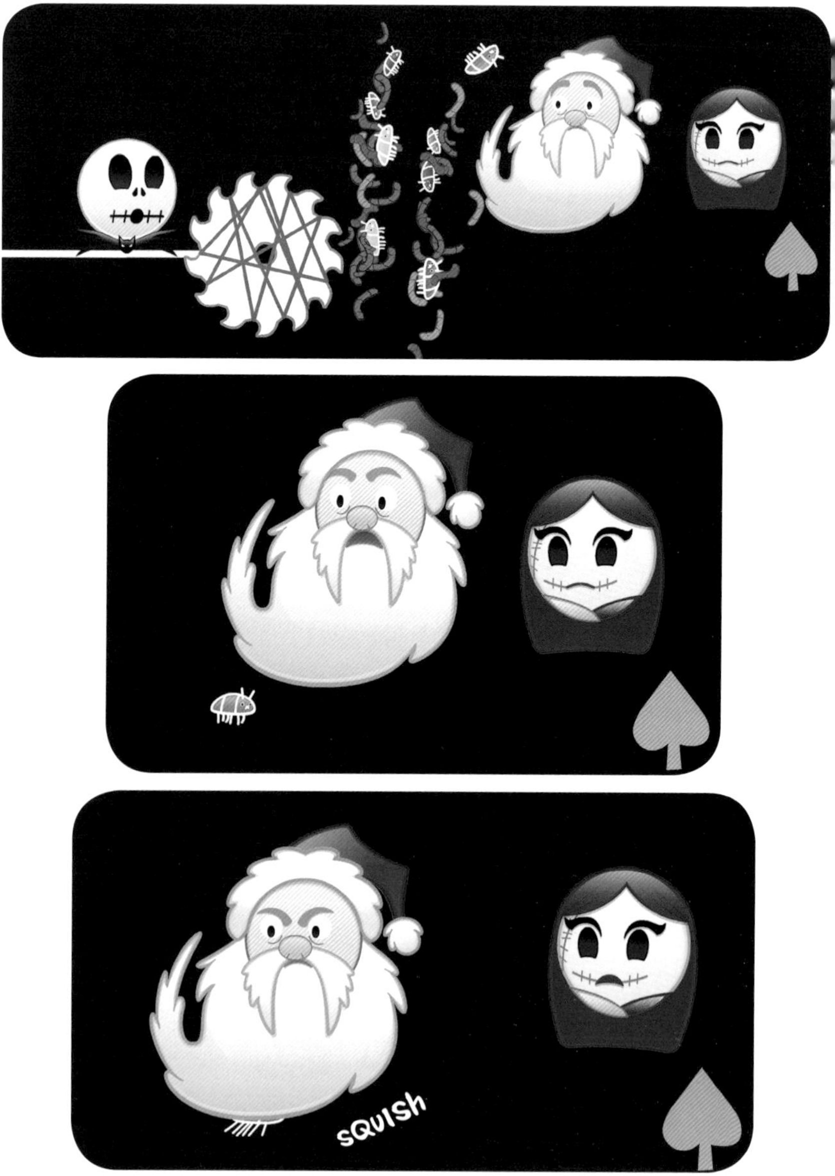
SQUISH

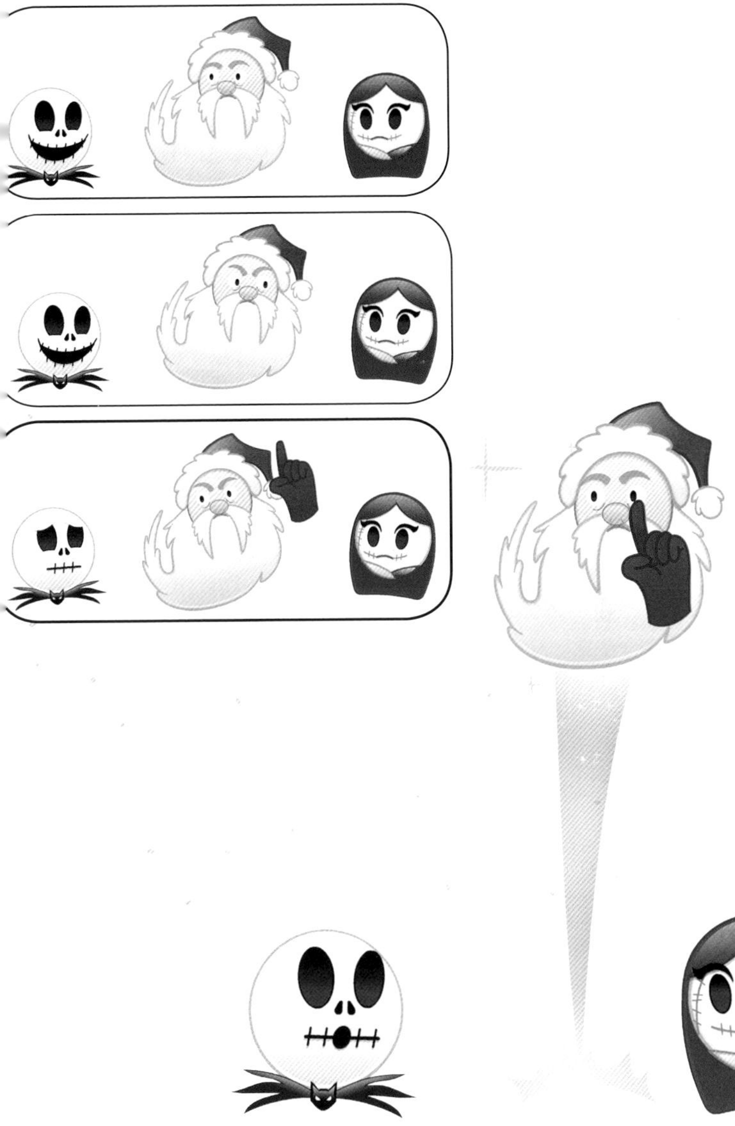

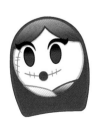

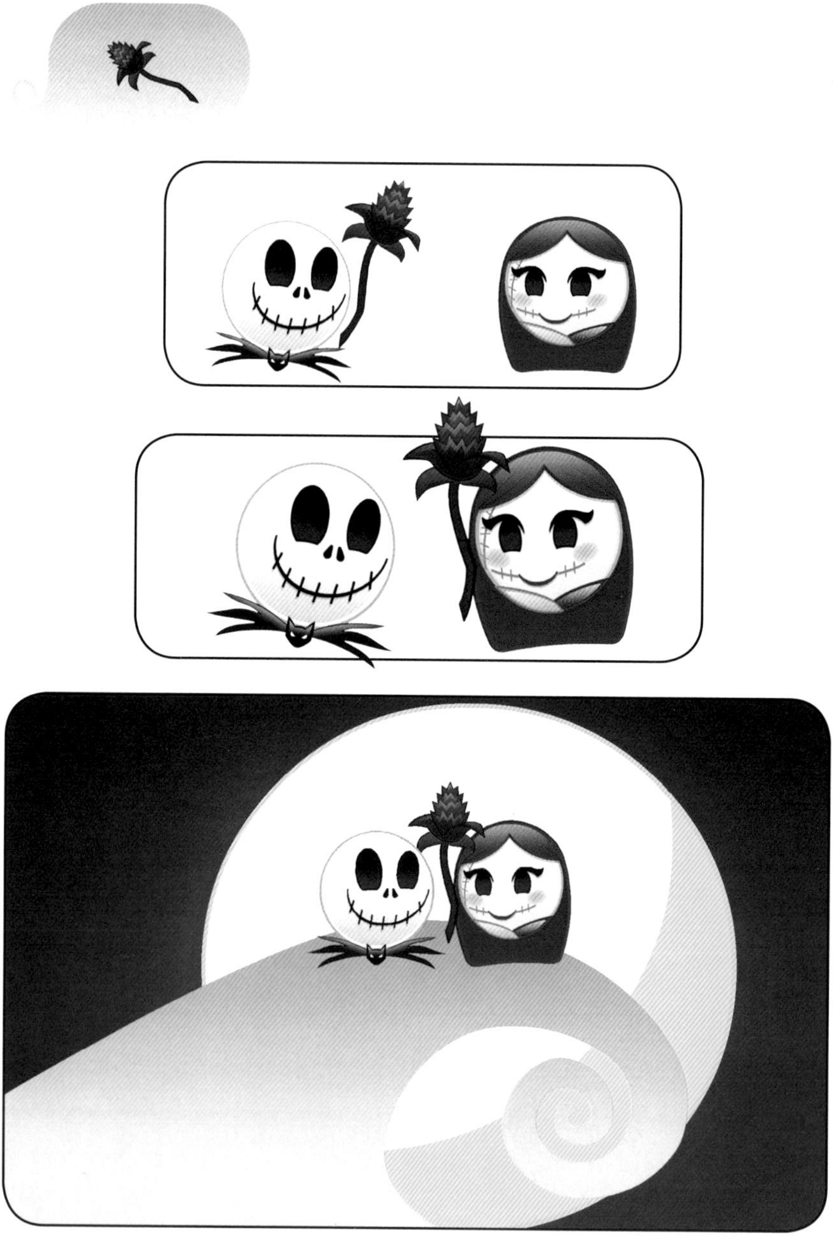

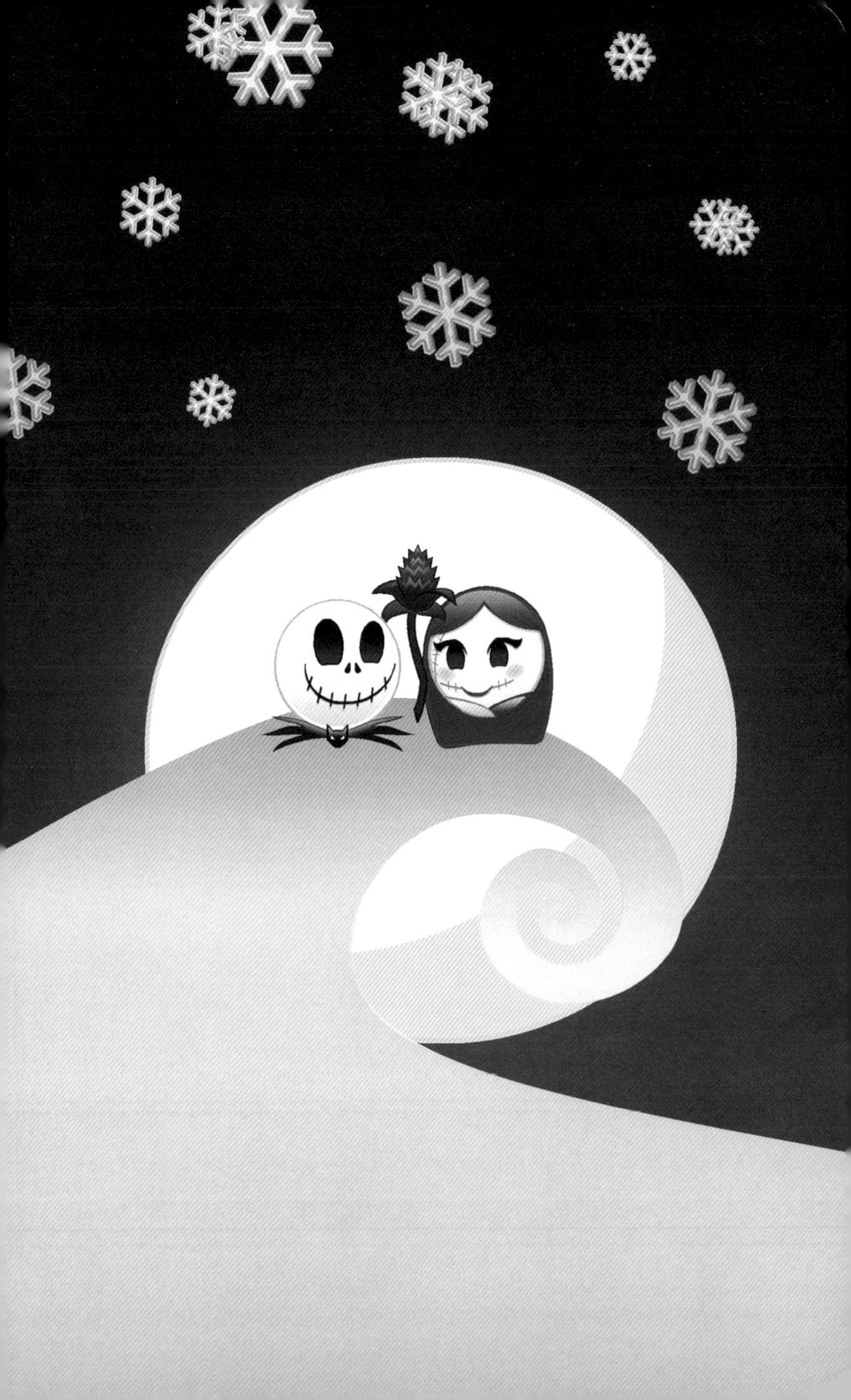

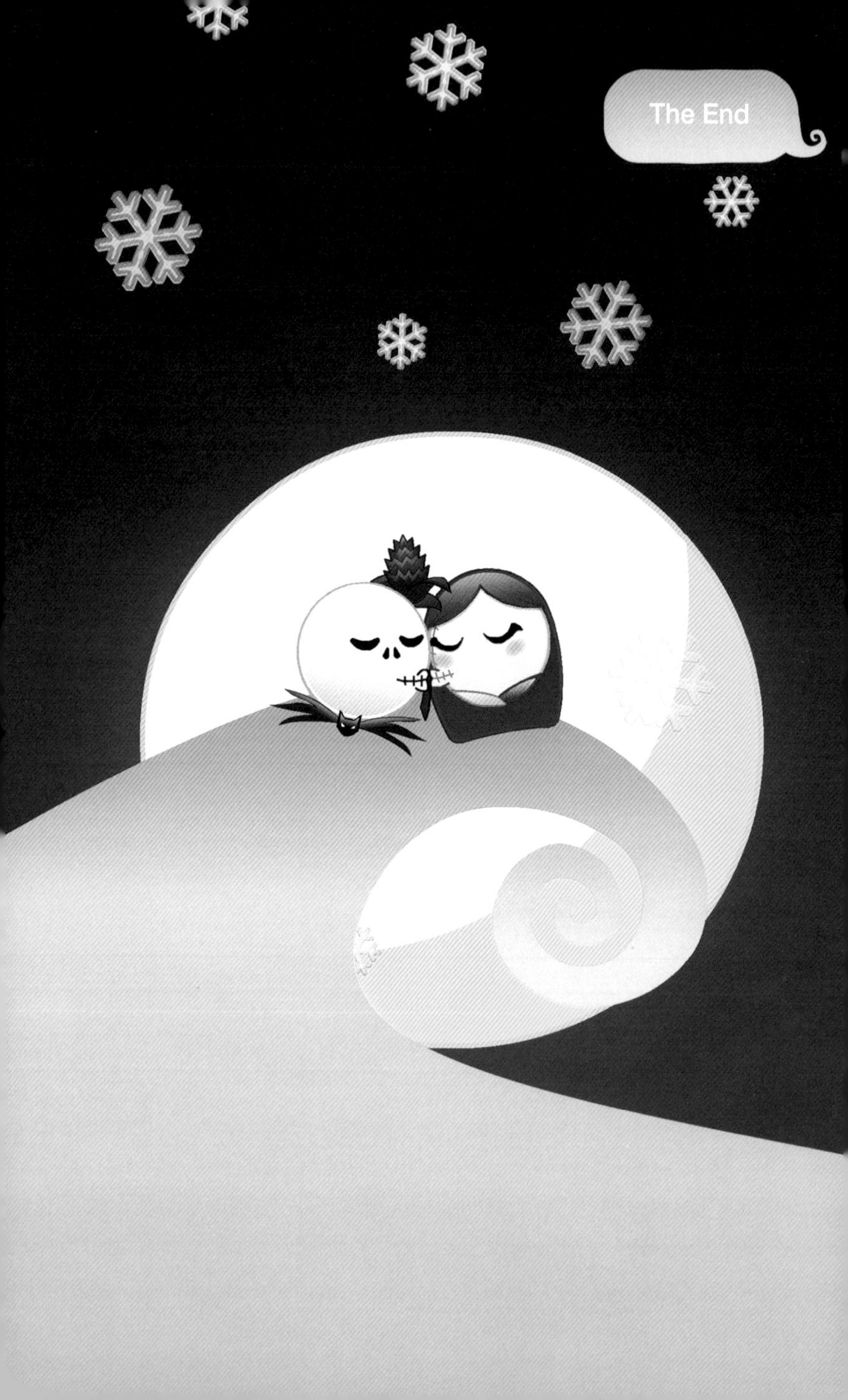
The End

Jack Skellington

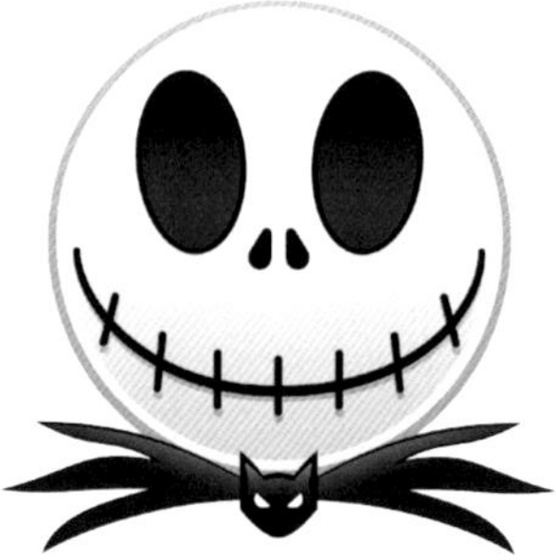

Jack Skellington is the of Halloween Town, in charge of bringing the world spooks and scares every October 31st.

Everything changes when discovers some place entirely new, Town, home of !

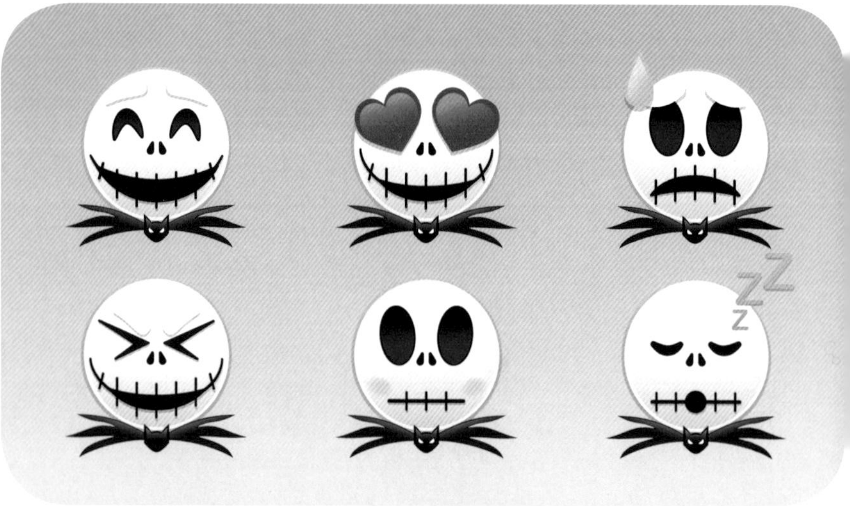

Sally

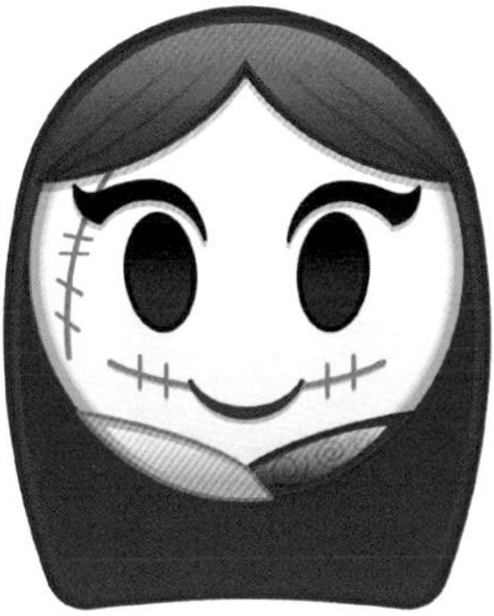

Sally—a shy, creative dreamer—is a rag doll created by the mad scientist .

 has trouble fitting in, but she has a very good friend in .

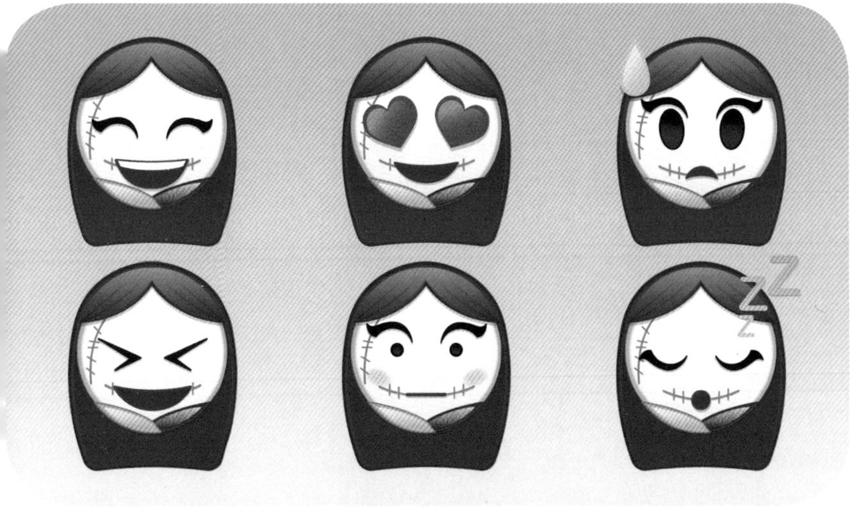

Zero is the ghost of a , and 's faithful friend.

On Christmas Eve, guides Jack's with his bright nose!

Oogie Boogie

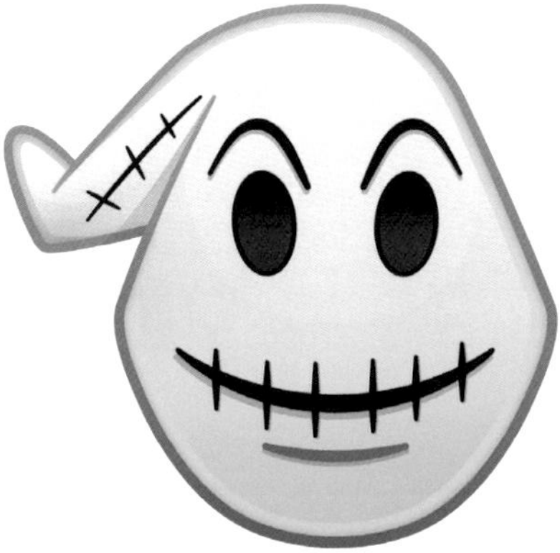

Oogie Boogie is a rambling, gambling bag of .

 is the not-so-welcoming host for 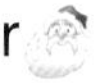 on Christmas Eve.

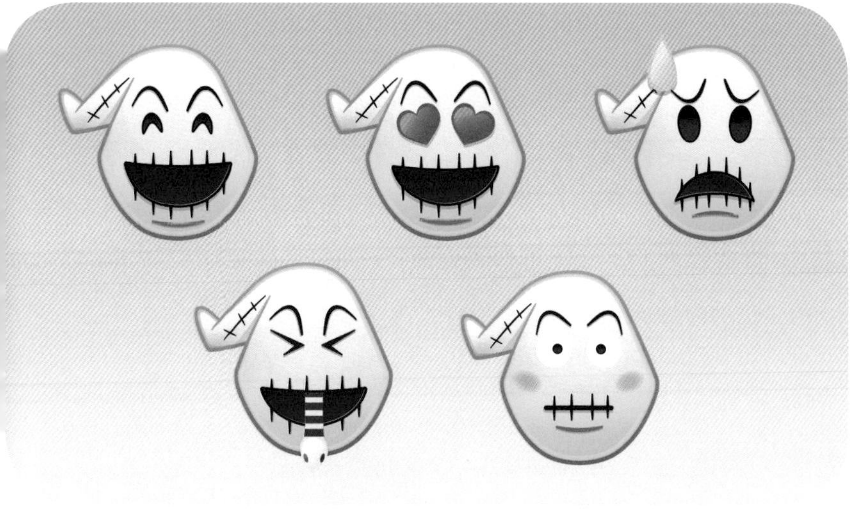

Sandy Claws

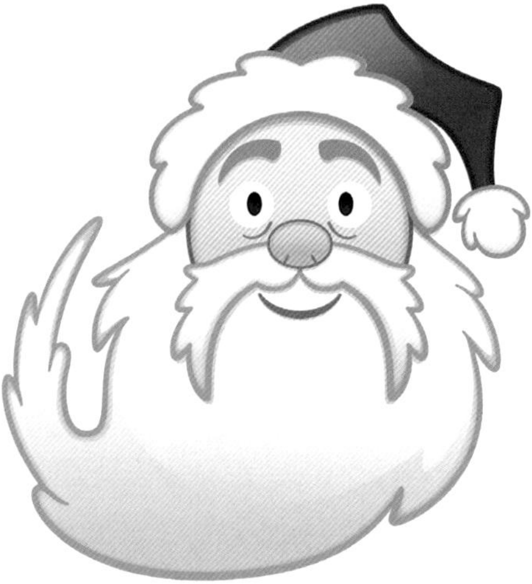

Christmas just isn't the same without this jolly old fellow, or so finds out the hard way.

fixes his holiday and spreads good cheer, bringing to the children of the world.

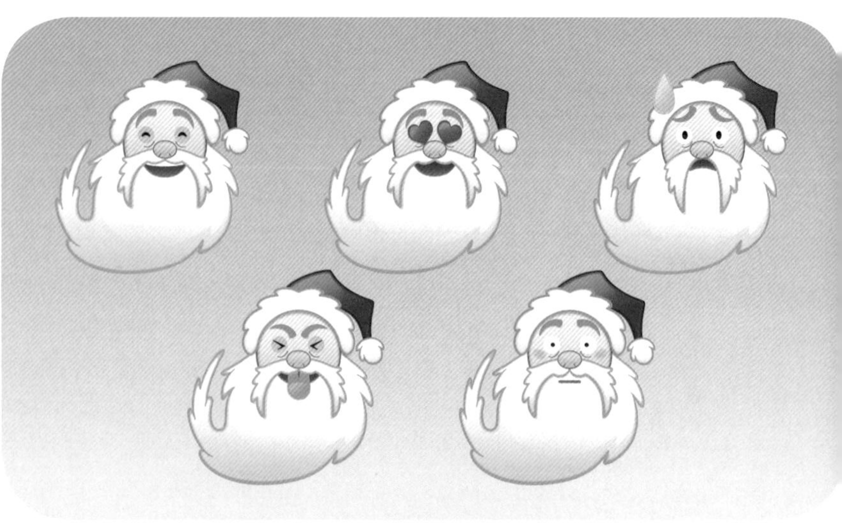

Mayor

You could call the Mayor of Halloween Town two-faced—literally! He is known for alternating between being 😧 and 😀, but he loves getting the town involved in 🎃 preparations.

Dr. Finkelstein

Dr. Finkelstein is the resident mad scientist of Halloween Town.

☺ created 🤖 so he would have an intelligent companion to spend time with.

Lock, Shock, and Barrel

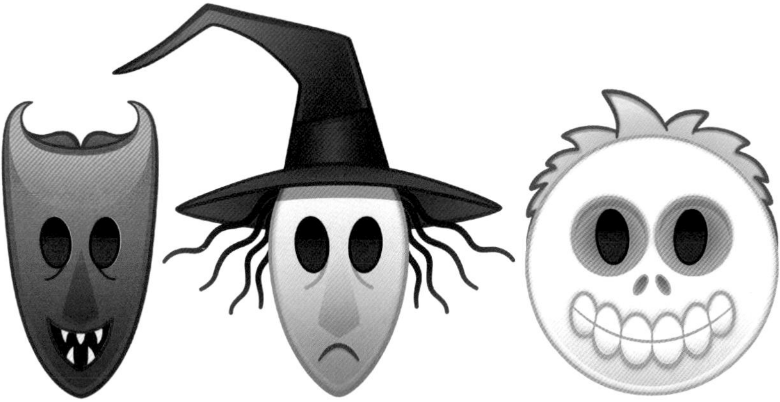

Lock, Shock, and Barrel are Halloween Town's trio of trick-or-treating troublemakers.

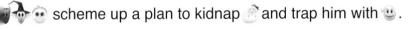

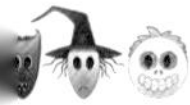 scheme up a plan to kidnap  and trap him with .

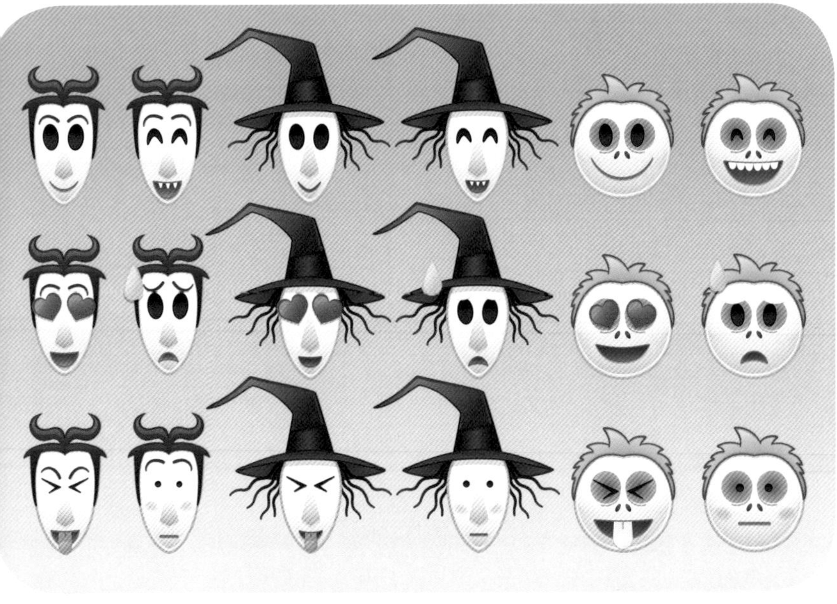

Collect them all!

As Told By Disney emoji

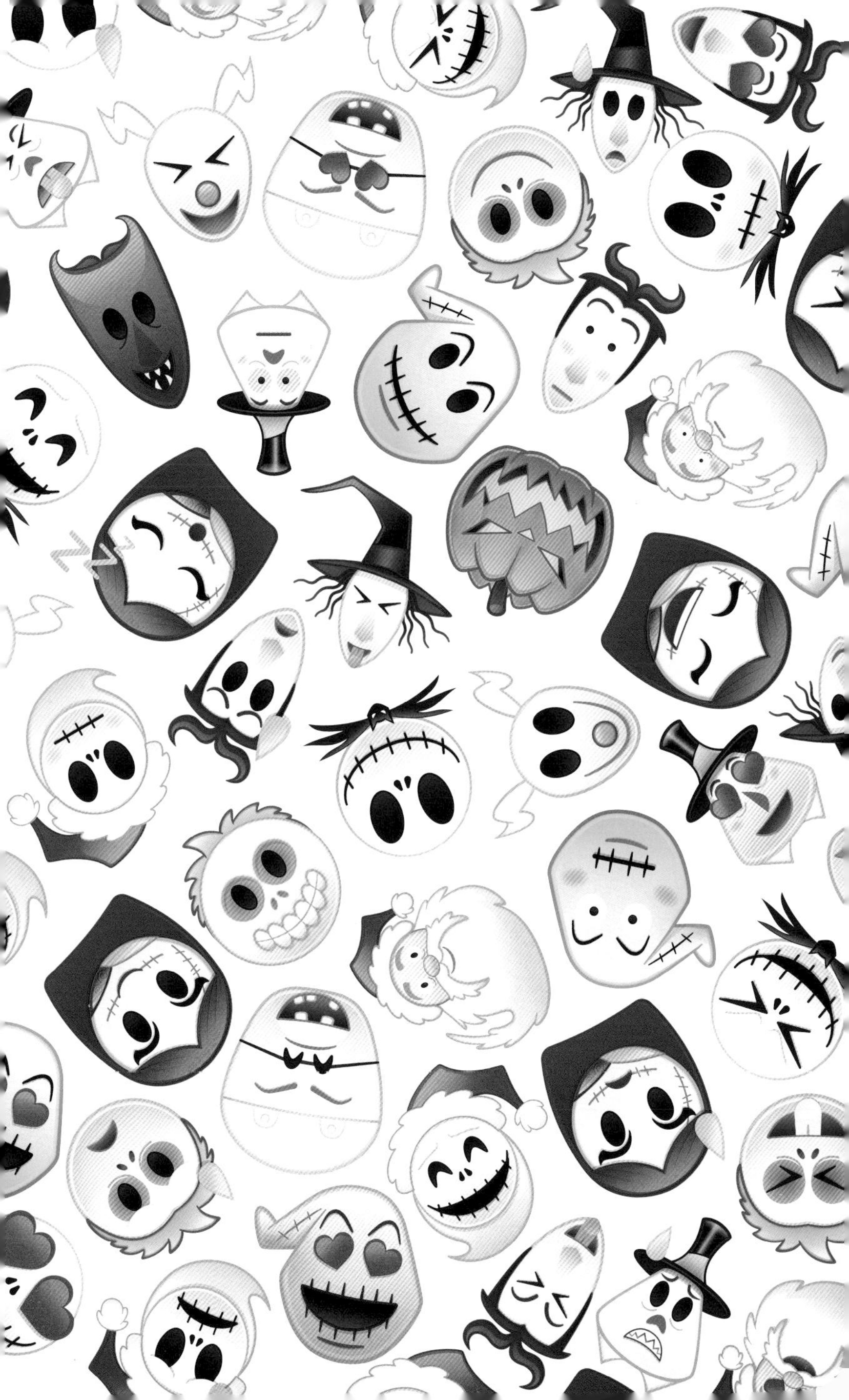

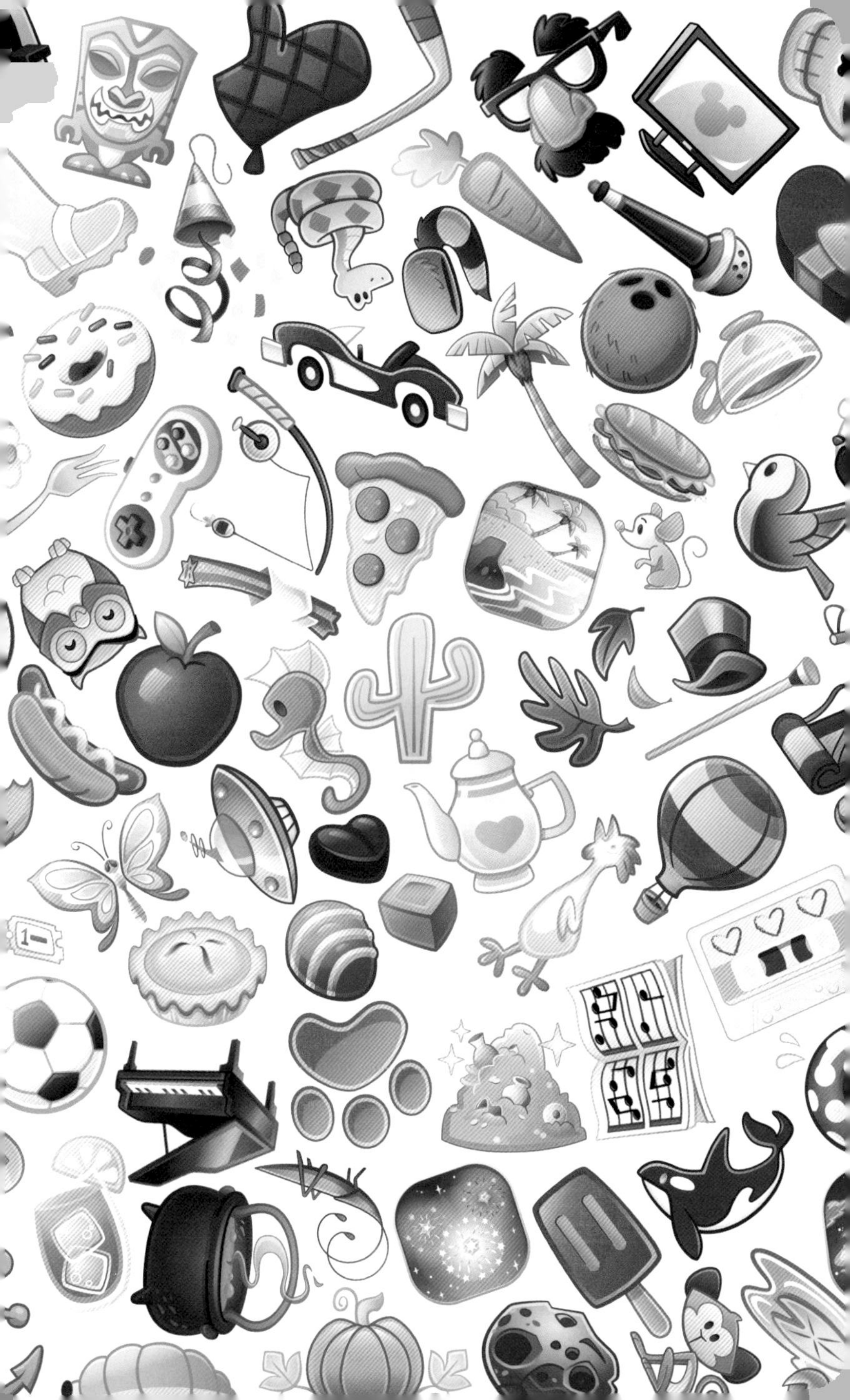

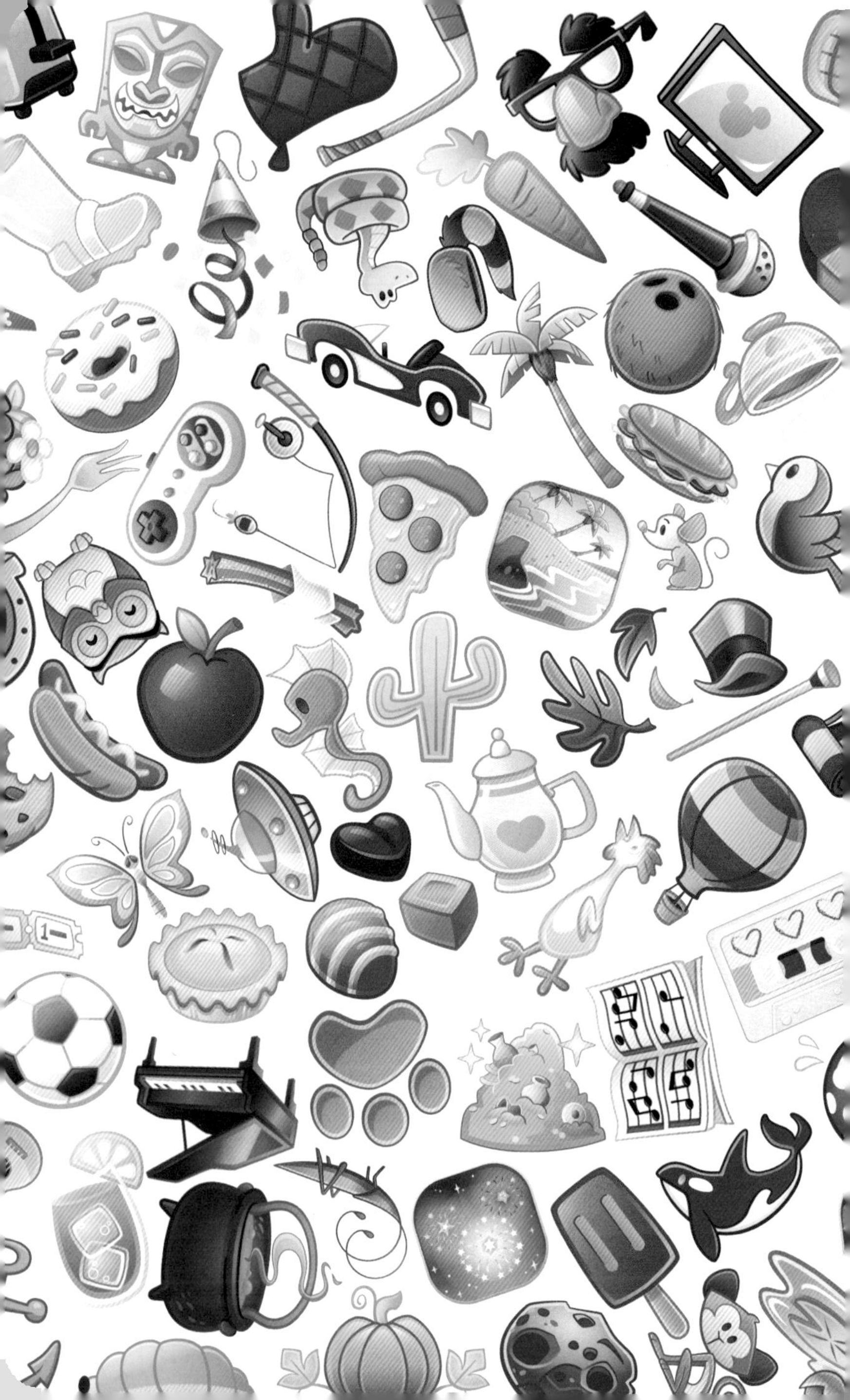